TEMBANI

IN

THE SILENT VOICE
THAT SPOKE THE LOUDEST

BY ROSE TK

First paperback edition 2023

978-1-7399100-6-8 (paperback)
978-1-7399100-4-4 (eBook)
978-1-7399100-9-9 (hardcover)

CONTENTS

CHAPTER ONE
Sindi and Pilani meet for the first time 1

CHAPTER TWO
Pilani and Sindi's love blossoms 5

CHAPTER THREE
A meeting with the future in-laws 11

CHAPTER FOUR
Sindi makes an unexpected decision 19

CHAPTER FIVE
A family is formed 29

CHAPTER SIX
Tembani is born 35

CHAPTER SEVEN
A surprise goes wrong 37

CHAPTER EIGHT
A trigger that changes their lives forever 41

CHAPTER NINE
Sindi makes a brave decision 53

CHAPTER TEN
*A new life for Sindi unfolds,
and a surprise reunion is on the cards*.. 65

CHAPTER ELEVEN
Tembani's childhood emotions are triggered................................77

CHAPTER TWELVE
Tembani reveals a deep secret.. 95

CHAPTER THIRTEEN
Mr Aloha observes Tembani's unusual behaviour 99

CHAPTER FOURTEEN
Mr Aloha, the advocate 105

CHAPTER FIFTEEN
Tembani shares good news 117

CHAPTER SIXTEEN
Tembani begins his school project.. 121

CHAPTER SEVENTEEN
A transformation that will mark history 127

CHAPTER EIGHTEEN
A transformation like no other 135

CHAPTER NINETEEN
Tembani, the unexpected entrepreneur 141

TEMBANI

CHAPTER TWENTY
Tembani transforms from boy to man 145

CHAPTER TWENTY-ONE
Tembani tells his story 153

CHAPTER TWENTY-TWO
Unfinished business 163

CHAPTER TWENTY-THREE
A significant meeting 171

CHAPTER TWENTY-FOUR
Long-awaited news for Sindi 179

CHAPTER TWENTY-FIVE
A foundation is launched 189

CHAPTER ONE

Sindi and Pilani meet for the first time

Once upon a time, a young, beautiful woman named Sindi lived on a council estate in a city called Westvale. She was 20 years of age and lived with her parents. She was the last of four children. She had three brothers who were all grown up and had left home to start their own families. Her family had immigrated to England from Africa many years ago. Sindi was less than two years old when her parents immigrated.

Her family did not have a lot of money, despite both her parents working two jobs each. Sindi had dropped out of school because of this. She enjoyed spending quality time with her mother, helping her with cooking and baking. Her mother was an excellent cook and baker, and Sindi had learnt these skills from her at a tender age.

Their house was located near a grocery shop named Mack's Mini Market, at which Sindi was a frequent shopper. One sunny afternoon, on her regular shopping trip, Sindi met a man who would change her life forever.

As she was walking along aisle 3, a section for tinned items, looking for coconut milk and other baking ingredients, she caught a glimpse of a tall and handsome man who was also looking for something next to her. Their eyes met, and Sindi's heart instantly started to beat faster. She quickly looked away as she did not want to show her feelings. She was normally very shy, and at that moment, she started to panic. She hastily tried to reach out for the coconut milk tin she wanted, but unfortunately, at five foot two, she was unable to reach it. The gentleman noticed this and just smiled.

Sindi started to tiptoe, making great efforts to stretch her hand out as far as she could to grab the tin, but she just couldn't reach it. The gentleman immediately walked towards Sindi and offered his assistance.

"Can I help? What can I get for you?" the man asked.

His voice was so deep, smooth and mesmerising.

"Hi...um...that one," she said, pointing at the tin of coconut milk. "Thanks," Sindi replied shyly. Inwardly, her emotions had started to race. She could not believe such a handsome man would offer his help to her.

The man placed his shopping basket on the floor, stretched his long arm to reach for the tin of coconut milk Sindi wanted and then gently handed it to her.

My, he's so handsome! She thought to herself but made an effort to disguise her feelings.

"You're such a gentleman. Thank you very much," she said shyly.

"The pleasure is all mine. By the way, my name is Pilani, and what is your name?" He stretched out his arm to shake Sindi's hand.

"Sindi is my name. Sindi with an 'S,' not 'C' as you would expect," she replied. She seemed in a hurry and wanted to walk away.

"Beautiful name, and nice to meet you, Sindi. So, you like coconut milk, hey?" Pilani asked with a smile.

"Yeah...Me and my mum like to use coconut milk in most of our cooking and baking," she replied.

"I see. I guess you are a great cook, then?" Pilani said.

"I am not too bad," Sindi replied with a smile, but inwardly, her heart was thumping so fast, as this was the first time she had spoken to a stranger in this shop.

"It was really nice to meet you, Pilani, but I have to go," Sindi said and started to walk briskly towards the till to pay for her shopping.

As she was about to leave the shop, Pilani followed her and shouted out, "Hey, Sindi, wait! Can I speak to you for a moment, please?"

Sindi stopped walking and looked back to face Pilani, who was just a heel behind her.

"Yeah?" she asked.

"Um...I just wanted to say you look so beautiful," Pilani said.

"O-kayyy, thanks," Sindi said but started to walk away again.

"Please, wait. Um...do you live around here?" Pilani asked.

"Mm, yeah. Why do you ask?"

"I come here a lot, and I have never seen you before, that's why."

"I guess we just come at different times."

"You seem like you are in such a big rush. Erm...I would like to get to know you. May I ask for your mobile number, please?" Pilani blurted all this out before Sindi got a chance to walk away.

"I don't give my number to strangers, thank you!" Sindi spoke firmly and turned her heels to make a quick getaway.

Pilani walked faster, too, as he was not ready to give up.

"Of course, I get that. Can I give you my number instead...please?" he asked Sindi.

His voice was breathtaking, and Sindi's heart was melting with admiration, but she just did not want to show it. She continued to play hard to get.

"Please," he said again, seemingly shy at this point.

"Okay, go on then."

Pilani let out an audible sigh of relief, and without wasting any time, he hastily slipped his laptop case off his shoulder and took out a notepad. He quickly jotted his mobile number down and handed it to Sindi.

She gave him a good look as if to suggest, 'Should I trust you?' but without hesitation, she stretched out her hand and accepted the number. She quickly shoved it into her handbag.

"Please don't lose that paper," Pilani said with a smile followed by a nervous chuckle.

Sindi just shrugged her shoulders as if to suggest that she didn't care, but of course she did.

"By the way, can I ask you something? Why are you carrying a rucksack and laptop bag?" Sindi asked Pilani.

"Oh! The bag has students' exercise books in it, and this bag has my laptop. I am a teacher at Bryanston Secondary School. You know it? The one on Watson Road."

"Oh, great! What do you teach, and what level?" she asked.

"Maths, to junior and senior level. So, what do you do?"

"Nothing. I don't work. I just help my mother around the house."

"I see. Can I get your number, please? Before you go? Just in case you lose mine?" Pilani was insistent, as he could not imagine not being able to see Sindi again. She had clearly taken his heart by surprise.

There is something special about her, he thought to himself.

This time, Sindi gave him her number because she, too, felt there was a strong connection between them.

Thanks, Sindi with an 'S'," Pilani said gently and with a cheeky smile. "Speak later?"

"Okay."

By the time Sindi arrived home, Pilani had already sent her a text.

[Hope you got home safe? Speak to you soon. Take care]

[I did, thanks. Looking forward xxx] Sindi replied.

A few more messages kept rolling in. Sindi giggled as she read the texts, like a schoolgirl in love for the first time. Her mum just watched reading the messages and smiling from ear to ear.

My daughter must be in love, she thought to herself. A mother's instinct kicked in, but she decided not to say anything to Sindi at this point. A memory of her younger self flashed in her thoughts.

CHAPTER TWO

Pilani and Sindi's love blossoms

From the day that Sindi and Pilani met in the grocery store, they met regularly at a local park. They had their favourite spot, a two-seater bench located there. When away from each other, they texted constantly. Since it was Sindi's first relationship, she felt very scared as she didn't know what to expect.

One day, as Sindi was cooking in the kitchen with her mum as they always did, Sindi was a bit fidgety than usual. She had been thinking deeply about confiding in her mum about her relationship. She couldn't bear to keep this a secret from her for much longer. Besides, she was her rock, and Sindi trusted her very much.

"Are you okay, Sindi? You've been a bit clumsy lately, and I notice you're even clumsier today. You keep dropping things all over the place. Are you alright?" her mum asked.

"I'm alright, Mum. But I have something I need to tell you, and please don't be mad at me."

"Mad at you? For what? You're scaring me already. What is it that you want to tell me?"

"How old were you when you met Dad?"

"I was about sixteen, I think, and he was seventeen. We met at high school. He was one grade ahead of me. Why do you ask?"

"Well, do you remember that day when you asked me to go to the grocery store to buy you a tin of coconut milk and ingredients to make your jollof rice?"

"Of course I still remember the day. What happened?"

Sindi's mum instantly figured out what her daughter was about to say based on her recent behaviour and a twinkle in her eyes. But she decided to keep these thoughts to herself for now.

"Mum, I kind of kept a little secret from you, and I feel bad. I met a man at Mack's Mini Mart grocery store, but the way we met was a bit strange."

"What do you mean?"

"You know they have a tendency at Mini Mack's to stack some items high up on their shelves?"

"Right. Is that the secret?"

"No, Mum, wait! Let me tell you what happened next. This lovely gentleman noticed that I was trying to reach for your tin of coconut milk, and he quickly came to help me." Sindi started smiling.

"And then what happened?"

"He then asked me for my name and followed me around the shop, asking me for my mobile number."

"Oh, that's so strange! This has never happened to you before, right? Did you feel scared?"

"Not at all, Mum. By the way, he didn't follow me in a creepy way, before you start telling me off."

"I hope you didn't tell him your name instantly, did you?" Sindi's mum asked with a concerned look.

"Mum, you're jumping the gun; let me finish my story. Of course, I told him my name. Listen to this: the moment our eyes met, my heart started to melt. I felt this unusual connection with him, Mum. He is about six foot three and *very* handsome, and to top this, he has these deep dimples, hmmmm..."

Sindi's mum closed her eyes with one hand. She couldn't believe it was her Sindi talking. This was so unlike her.

"Don't close your eyes, Mum, there's still more. After I told him my name, he wouldn't give up pursuing me. I don't think he bought everything that he wanted because he didn't want to lose *moi*."

"Since when do you speak French?" her mum said, laughing.

"He really tried so hard, and I eventually gave in and gave him my number. He was just too good-looking for me to let him go." Sindi giggled. "And I will be meeting him again next week. He asked me on a date. So what do you think?"

"What do I think? Everything just seems so dramatic. The question is, what do you think?"

"I would like to meet him again, see how the date goes, and I will take it from there: when I know whether I really like him or not."

"What is his name, and what does he do?"

"He told me his name is Pilani, and he's a maths teacher at Bryanston Secondary School near Gumspree Park."

"Oh, that one. That's interesting. Well, Sindi, you're twenty years of age, and I'm sure you know your wrongs from right, especially on your first date. I just want you to be safe and not be too trusting at this stage. Please meet each other in a public place for your first few dates, and no..."

Sindi immediately interrupted her mum; she knew exactly what she was going to say. "Yes, Ma, I know, I know. I won't do any of that. In fact, he invited me for a meal at Laylas."

"Oh, that's alright then. Let me know how the date goes."

If Sindi had supernatural powers, she would have fast-forwarded the time. She could not wait for Saturday to meet Pilani. On the day, she picked up more than six outfits and piled them in a heap on her bed. She couldn't decide which one to wear for her first date, but eventually chose to dress in a lovely colourful long frock, and she made an effort to braid her hair and put a few beads in it.

Pilani was already waiting for her at Laylas, and as soon as his eyes met Sindi's, he couldn't help but grin from ear to ear. He was pleased with what he saw.

"You look stunning," Pilani complemented Sindi.

Smiling, she replied, "Thanks. You look good, too."

Pilani behaved like a true gentleman. He stood up to pull back Sindi's chair for her to sit down and then gently slid it forward after she sat. Sindi was so impressed.

What a gentleman; I feel like a princess, she thought to herself.

The date went very well; the pair giggled non-stop. They talked about their hobbies, families and when they would meet again.

At the end of their meal, Pilani said, "Thank you for making this day so special for me, Sindi. Days like this don't come easy." Pilani reached his hand out across the table to hold her hand.

"You reckon?" she said as she smiled.

Sindi was a bit tense, but she still allowed Pilani to hold her hand; besides, she felt safe as there were other people around.

"You look prettier each time I look at you."

"Oh, come on, stop flattering me," she said, becoming shy.

"I mean it. Your smile is so gorgeous. I hope I will meet you again soon. Let me call a taxi for you," he said.

"A taxi? What for? I'll get the bus. I'll be alright, but thanks for the offer. By the way, thanks for inviting me," Sindi said with a soft tone to her voice.

"You're most welcome," Pilani replied.

As Sindi was about to stand up from her chair, Pilani gave her the same honour, gently pulling her chair out with one hand and placing the other behind his back. Pilani behaved like a true gentleman, and Sindi was impressed.

"Before you go," he said, "I would like to say that we've been seeing each other for a little while now. I think I would like to move our relationship forward a little bit more. I would like to meet your family, if that's okay with you, and maybe get to taste your cooking, which I have no doubt will be amazing."

"I'll have a think about that, and I will get back to you. Don't you think you're moving too swiftly?" Sindi said, playing hard to get.

"Well, I'll wait as long as it takes if I have to," Pilani said with a gentle smile.

There was a warm feeling from both of them. Their connection was undoubtedly incredible.

Sindi could not wait to get home and tell her mother about how her date had gone.

When she got home, she looked for her mum around the house, breathing heavily.

"Hey, what's with that look? How did the date go?" Sindi's mum asked.

"Mum, I'm in love. Pilani is the loveliest person I have ever met. He treated me like a princess today. The food at the restaurant was amazing, and we giggled like school kids and people around us were just staring at us as if judging us."

"Oh, that's great news. I'm glad you still feel the same about him. So when will you be seeing him again?"

"In fact, he has asked to meet you. Is it too early, Mum?" Sindi asked with a wink.

"Sindi, you literally met this man a few months ago. Do you think you know him well enough to introduce him to us? I know it's your first love, but I think you are rushing things a bit, and I think you need to take your time to get to know him. Those are my thoughts."

"Mum, please!"

"Okay, okay. When he's ready to come, let me know so that I can tell your father to be home too. I would need to tidy the house, and we'd need to get ingredients to make our special dishes."

"In actual fact, he is actually looking forward to tasting *my* cooking."

"You mean *our* cooking? That way, he will not be disappointed for sure."

They both shared a good laugh.

Sindi took off her heels, put on comfortable shoes and helped her mum to make their dinner.

CHAPTER THREE
A meeting with the future in-laws

Sindi and Pilani's relationship moved swiftly, one thing leading to another. They were so love-smitten from the start and would not let any delays come in the way of their relationship.

On one of their dates, Sindi suggested the best time for Pilani to meet her mum. She was not comfortable bringing him to her family home when her father was around. He was a very strict man and would not meet anyone unless they were ready to propose. However, she did not tell Pilani this as she did not want to insinuate anything to him.

"Are you ready to meet my mother soon?" Sindi asked Pilani.

"Of course. I have always been ready; I was just waiting for the cue from you. But you know what? If I'm honest with you, I feel pretty nervous. I hope she will be nice to me. What should I wear? A suit and tie?" Pilani said.

"Oh, please, no. Don't dress like you're going for a job interview!" She laughed. "Just dress normally, like smart/casual, and of course, my mum will be nice to you. What do you take her for? But, there's just one more thing you should know to keep you on top of things."

"What's that?"

"Please, I beg you, don't eat anything before you come to my house. My mum has a reputation for serving big meals. Don't feel ashamed to finish everything she serves you if you like her food, which I am confident you will."

"You're very cheeky. Let's see what happens on the day." Pilani smiled.

When Sindi got home, she informed her mum of her intention to introduce Pilani to her.

"I know I said I don't mind meeting him, but I'm just sceptical that you've not known this man for that long, Sindi," her mum said.

"I know, Mum, but I'm truly in love. I just know he is the one. You will see what I mean when you meet him. He's handsome, tall, smart, a gentleman and has dimples: basically, just everything I want in my ideal man. His voice, my word, will make you melt, Mum!"

"Oh, behave yourself; don't let your father hear you say that. Don't you think you're rushing things a bit? Slow down and give yourselves time to know each other well."

"Mum, please don't burst my bubble."

"I'm just saying."

"I hear you, Mum, don't stress. There's nothing to worry about."

She shared a joke or two with her mum whilst they continued cooking in the kitchen, and they were very close.

Sindi just giggled, and in her mind, she had made the decision that Pilani was the right man for her.

That day finally arrived when Sindi introduced Pilani to her mother. She and her mum had spent half the day running around like headless chickens, making efforts to impress Pilani. They were unsure of what to prepare for him and had gone out of their way to buy a lot of ingredients, making use of the buy-one-get-one-free deals.

When Pilani arrived at Sindi's house, he knocked on the door.

"Come on in, and please take a seat over there," Sindi's mother said. "My word, you're tall!" she said. She suddenly remembered what Sindi had told her.

Pilani just smiled and inwardly convinced himself *Sindi's mum likes me.*

"I guess you're the Pilani my daughter has been talking about non-stop?" she said.

"Yes, Ma, I am. How are you?"

"I'm good, Son. First things first, can I offer you a hot or cold drink?"

"Hmmm…Water will do, Ma."

She collected a bottle of water from the fridge and handed it to Pilani.

Sindi sat next to Pilani on their two-seater sofa, and her mum sat on a single seat just further away from the pair.

"Right, Pilani, I am of an old generation type, and I will ask you some uncomfortable questions. I hope you will not mind."

"That's okay, Ma." Pilani smiled nervously as he was not sure what questions Sindi's mum was going to ask him.

Sindi just closed her eyes. She knew her mum would not hold back on her questioning.

"So, tell me, what attracted you to my daughter? You are her first boyfriend, and I need to make one thing very clear to you from the beginning. I am a very protective mother. Sindi is still a young woman in my eyes, and I would not want to see her hurt in any shape or form."

"I understand that, Ma. I guess that's what every parent would do. Well, to answer your question, I was attracted to your daughter because she is a very beautiful young lady and I love her very much. I loved her the very first time I met her at the grocery store."

"I am very sorry to ask you again a rather personal question. How old are you?" she asked.

"I am 30 years of age."

"Are you aware Sindi is only 20 years of age? There is a clear big gap between you."

"I am aware of that, Ma. She told me."

"Why did it take you this long to settle down?"

Pilani swallows a large gulp of saliva, not really sure of how to answer the question.

"I guess I was waiting for the right woman to come along, and I believe your daughter is *that* woman."

Sindi smiled shyly.

"So, do you live around Westvale?"

"Yes, Ma. I own a council house along Pentagon Street."

"I see. Anyway, I will leave you two for now, and it was nice to meet you. By the way, a meal has been prepared for you, and Sindi will serve you shortly. I will see you before you leave."

"Thank you, Ma."

After Sindi had served Pilani, based on his reaction, licking all his fingertips and wiping his plate squeaky clean using all his fingers, he asked Sindi if she was as good a cook as her mum.

"We both prepared the meal, dah," she joked.

As always, they share a laugh.

Pilani stayed briefly after eating and thanked both Sindi and her mother for preparing a tasty meal for him. Before he bid them farewell, he promised he would keep in touch. As Pilani was walking out, Sindi asked him a question he did not expect at that time.

"Hey, babe, so when am I going to meet your family?" she asked.

"First of all, I am not comfortable with you calling me 'babe.' Where did you learn that? I guess I am too old-fashioned. I would prefer you call me by my actual name or something better than 'Babe,' alright? To answer your question, I will introduce you to my family soon."

"How soon?"

"Patience, Miss, have patience, I said very soon. Leave it with me," he responded sharply.

However, Sindi did not even pay attention to Pilani's tone of voice. She was too mesmerised by him at this time.

A month passed by before Pilani invited Sindi to meet his family. One day, unexpectedly, she received a text from Pilani that made her feel very excited.

[Hi Si, when will you be available to meet my family?]

[When you're ready to invite me, I'll make myself available, dear. In fact, I can't wait for this day to come.]

[Really? That's great to know. I'll let you know soon of the suitable date, okay?]
[Can't wait. Speak to you soon xxxx]

She was very pleased that Pilani had eventually made this decision; to her, it seemed she had waited forever.

[Thanks for inviting me. So what am I expected to wear? Traditional or English attire?] she texted.

[My parents are very traditional people; I reckon if you wore a traditional dress, they'd be pleased.]

[I can't wait for this day. I'm so excited. I have to shop for the dress.]

[Enough of this texting. See you after work, same place.]

[Okay, later xxx]

After work, Pilani arranged to meet up with Sindi at their usual place on a bench situated at Gumspree Park.

Sindi was already at the park, waiting for him to come. When he finally arrived, he gave Sindi a hug and kiss.

"Hey, how was your day, my love?" Sindi asked.

"Pretty good. Today, all of my students were writing their mid-term maths test, so I was busy marking all day, and you? What were you doing all day? Don't tell me – cooking?" Pilani giggled.

"You think you know me too well now, don't you? In actual fact, I was busy doing laundry and ironing AND not cooking, hello!"

"Okay, I get it, I get it, Miss Know-it-all. I guess I got it wrong this time," he teased.

"Are you going to apologise then?"

"Sindisiwe, I AM SORRY! Happy now?"

"Yes, Sir! I am happy."

They both share a laugh.

Pilani then changed the topic and asked Sindi how she was preparing for his family visit.

"I hope you are not expecting a big feast prepared for you when you come to my house. If you're thinking along those lines, you will be disappointed. My family is not like that. In fact, I forgot to tell you something: my mum travelled back home a few days ago, and my father will definitely not have that time to cook for you."

Sindi looks at Pilani with one eye closed as if to say, *'Are you joking?'*

"Don't even look at me like that. I can't even make toast, so don't even think about it."

"It's okay, my love." Sindi took hold of Pilani's hand and started to swing it about like a little child. "All I want is to meet your family. I've always wondered, who amongst your parents is tall?"

"It's my father; he's the taller one. My mum's height is pretty average. She's about five foot eight, and I guess for a lady that's pretty tall. But I'm slightly taller than my father, though, by some inches."

"Oh really, that is so amazing! I can't wait to meet my future in-laws."

"Soon," Pilani responded.

The day finally arrived when Sindi went to visit Pilani's family. Earlier, she had spent hours choosing which outfit would be most appropriate for the occasion. She eventually decided to wear a royal blue long dress with little patterns of butterflies, a matching necklace and headgear.

When she entered the house, Pilani's father was the one who opened the door, and he gazed at her from head to toe as if judging her outfit. Sindi was surprised by this reaction. She felt so unwelcome and uncomfortable, but she had to be brave for the occasion and not let this observation put her off this early on in her visit, let alone in their relationship.

"Hello, Sir. How are you?" Sindi extended her arm to greet Pilani's father, but this gesture was not reciprocated. *How rude,* she thought.

"Is this how you greet your elders where you come from? You don't curtsy for your elders?" he asked rudely.

For a moment, Sindi was lost for words, but she managed to keep her cool composure. "I'm sorry, Sir," she apologised.

"Take a seat over there," he said, speaking sharply and pointing at a large sofa situated further away from him.

"Thank you, Sir."
They all sat down and Pilani made the introductions.
"Dad, please meet my girlfriend, Sindi, and Sindi, please meet my father, Mr Malunga."
"Nice to meet you, Sir, erm…sorry, Mr Malunga," Sindi stammered.
"Hmmm…First things first, what do you do for a living, Sindi?"
"I…I…don't work, Sir. I just help my mother in the house."
"Hmmm…interesting." He looked sternly in Pilani's direction as if to say I am disappointed in you. "I guess I will have a word with my son. But a pleasure to meet you, erm…your name again?"
"Sindisiwe, Sir, but many people prefer to call my name in short as Sindi."
"What does your name mean?"
"It means, 'We have been saved,' Sir."
"Oh, okay, Sindi, make yourself comfortable. There is a drink in the fridge and some nibbles if you're hungry. Feel free to serve yourself. Pilani's mother travelled, and there is no woman to cook for you today."
No woman to cook? This is ridiculous. Hmmm…He regards cooking as only a woman's chore? I hope Pilani does not have such a mindset, Sindi thought.
"No problem, Sir; I am not hungry at all, but thank you for the offer."
The atmosphere was so awkward. They all sat in silence for some time, and this made Sindi feel even more uncomfortable. During her visit, she noticed that Pilani and his father barely spoke to each other and did not make eye contact. Their relationship just seemed very strange for a father and son.
Is it because of my presence, or is there more to their relationship I am yet to discover? raced in her mind.
Sindi could not wait to leave as she found the visit very unwelcoming and uncomfortable.
"So, where do you live, Sindi? Do you have siblings?" Pilani's father asked.

"I live in Chestnut Crescent near 'Mack's Mini Market,' and yes, Sir, I have three older brothers. I'm the only girl and the youngest."

"What do you want to do in the future if you marry my son? Just sit at home and have many children for him to look after?"

"I don't know about that, Sir. I really can't answer your question."

Sindi felt humiliated and very uncomfortable. She found his line of questioning derogatory. She could not wait to leave. This is not what she expected.

"Pilani, I promised Mum I'd be back soon. Sir, It was a real pleasure to meet you, but I have to go now. My mother would like me to help her in the house."

"Okay, Sindi. Greetings to your family, and I hope to see you again soon."

Over my dead body. I don't think so, she thought to herself.

Pilani and Sindi left the house. As they were walking, Pilani asked Sindi a question.

"So, what are your thoughts about my father?" he asked.

"Interesting man, I should say. He came across as very judgemental about people who are not educated, I thought. Does he expect everyone to be as educated as him?"

"What you witnessed there is nothing; I guess one day you will understand where I am coming from," he said.

Sindi certainly had a lot of unanswered questions about what she had just witnessed.

CHAPTER FOUR

Sindi makes an unexpected decision

It did not take long before Pilani decided to finally propose to Sindi. He planned this surprise very well. He decided not to inform any members of his family or Sindi's family. He thought it was their relationship and did not value the need to ask for a hand in marriage from her father as is always done traditionally. They were grown up, and according to Pilani, the decision to be together was between the two of them.

For this special occasion, he invited Sindi to a posh five-star restaurant called The Rosario. He planned for the staff to serve Sindi a champagne glass with the ring inside. When Pilani told Sindi about the venue of their date, she became miserable. This was not her; she was not used to going to expensive places, and anything of this nature made her feel uncomfortable.

"Do we have to go to that restaurant? How about us going to Chicken Inn?" she suggested.

"Come on, Sindi, this is a special date. I know it's your first time going there but don't worry, you will be fine. Trust me, I will look after you, and you won't feel out of place," Pilani reassured her.

Sindi always felt she did not deserve to be treated in a special way as she came from a poor background.

Pilani bought her a beautiful evening dress to wear for the occasion.

When Sindi took out the dress from the box Pilani had given her, she could not believe how lucky she was to have found a man like him. A tear of happiness dribbled down her cheek.

Why do I feel this is too good to be true? she thought to herself.

Whilst she was going through these emotions, her phone beeped, and it was Pilani, texting her to find out if she would get to the restaurant on time.

[*I'll be there in an hour. See you soon xxx*] she texted back.

Sindi made her way to the restaurant using the fastest route. She caught a number 943 bus and got off at the nearest tube station to get to the city centre. On the tube, everyone kept staring at her, which made her feel even more uncomfortable. She could not wait to get off at Bloomsbury Park station, where the restaurant was only two minutes away. Sindi took her time to walk as she did not want to sweat and ruin her make-up.

When she got to the restaurant, she was met by a waiter who was waiting for guests at the entrance and ushered to where Pilani was. He was wearing a black suit and a bow tie.

Why is he dressed like that? Sindi thought. *I hope it's not what I'm imagining.*

Pilani stood up, gave Sindi a hug and kept his gentlemanlike behaviour, causing her to feel respected as a woman once more. She also noticed that there were rose petals sprinkled all over their table, and when she looked around, other tables were not the same.

As soon as Sindi had settled down in her seat, the waiter quickly attended to them and asked her for her choice of drink. She chose orange juice.

"Come on, Sindi, this is a special night for us; choose a type of wine," Pilani said.

"A type of wine? Hmmm…" Sindi tapped her fingers on her chin. "I don't know any wine names." She giggled with embarrassment. "Can you help me to choose, please? Anything soft and not too heavy, thanks," she spoke softly.

"Waiter! Can I have a soft pink Rosse, please? Nice and chilled, please?" Pilani said.

"Yes, Sir," the waiter responded.

What Sindi didn't know was that Pilani had already planned for the restaurant staff to place an engagement ring at the bottom of the wine glass.

As the waiter served Sindi, she was busy looking around, mesmerised by her surroundings. The lighting was meticulous, and she felt great but certainly out of place.

As Sindi had a first sip of her wine, she started to cough. She was not familiar with the taste of the wine.

"Take your time, darling. You should take small sips," Pilani suggested.

"Okay, I...I...I'm not used to this." She smiled but was feeling a little embarrassed.

"It's okay; there's always a first time for everything, I guess," Pilani said.

As Sindi was about to finish her sparkling drink, she had still not noticed a ring at the bottom of the glass. Pilani had to act quickly before she swallowed it.

"Sindi, we have been dating for a few months now and introduced each other to our families," he said.

"I know, right? It's so surreal," she responded.

"I invited you here for a special occasion," Pilani said.

"I get it; this is so over the top."

"Of course – for a special person."

As Sindi was busy concentrating on Pilani, she had not noticed people slowly gathering around at a distance, as preplanned by Pilani.

Pilani got on one knee and said the magic words. "Sindi, will you marry me?"

She was in utter shock and nearly choked on her wine again. She held her hand to her mouth in disbelief.

Wow! Things are surely moving fast, she thought.

"YES! Yes, I will marry you!" she quickly responded.

Sindi saw Pilani put his fingers in her drink, and she blurted out, "What are you doing?"

She then became speechless when she saw him taking out a sparkling ring from her glass.

"Come on...was this ring in my glass all along?"

"Yes, I had to propose quickly before you swallowed it!" he said.

Sindi just giggled and gave Pilani a happy slap on his shoulders.

There was a large round of applause from other guests and the restaurant staff. They moved closer to their table and congratulated them on this new chapter in their lives.

At the end of their date, Pilani offered again to get a taxi for Sindi to drive her home. On this occasion, she did not refuse. Her heels were hurting her feet, she'd drunk some wine, plus it was a little late, and she did not want to get into trouble with her parents, especially her mum.

How will I break this news to Mum? I hope she will not be disappointed, Sindi imagined.

When she got home, the first thing she did was to take off her heels so that she would not make any noise. She tried opening the door as quietly as she could, but this did not work. The door squeaked, and her mother, who was sitting in the lounge watching television, jumped. Besides, she had been anxiously waiting for her to return.

"Sindi, what time do you call this?" she asked.

"Sorry, Mum, I...I was delayed. There was a lot of traffic."

"Don't give me those silly excuses. Just because you are twenty years of age doesn't make you safe. You were getting me worried there." She told Sindi off.

As her mum was talking, Sindi quickly removed her ring and placed it in her handbag as she did not want her mother to see it.

I'll tell her about this another time.

Sindi could sense that her mum was not happy with her, so she gave her a goodnight kiss on the cheek.

"Goodnight, Mum," she said.

"Night, Sindi," her mum responded.

That night, Sindi struggled to sleep, thinking about how she would break the news to her family that she accepted Pilani's proposal without their knowledge or approval.

A few weeks went by, and one Sunday afternoon, as they sat in the lounge watching television, Sindi decided to break the news to her mother.

"Mum, can I talk to you about something important? You need to sit down," Sindi said, and her heart started to thump.

"Yes, Sindi. What is it?"

"Mum, I'm engaged."

Her mum nearly choked on the tea she was sipping. "Excuse me? What do you mean you're engaged without the knowledge of me or your father? Are you out of your mind? Is this Pilani man driving you madly in love so you forget your roots? I am utterly disappointed in you, Sindi. I did not expect this from you at all!" she blurted out.

"But, Mum, I am twenty years old and can make my own decisions, and I...I..."

"I...I, what, Sindi? If you think being twenty years old means you can behave like that, then you will leave my house and go and live alone where no one can tell you what to do. Your behaviour right now is out of order, do you hear me? This is not what we do in our culture. You don't do things like that without the approval of your parents. Do I make myself clear?" she said.

This was the first time their mother-and-daughter relationship had been tested.

Sindi started to cry.

"I'm sorry for raising my voice at you," her mum said softly, "but I have to be honest that I am very disappointed in you. This is not how I raised you. Now tell me, how will I break this news to your father? You know for sure he will hit the roof, and I am really dreading that moment."

"Mum, I just can't take this anymore. I am going to my room and need some time to myself. Please don't come into my room," Sindi said with a sad tone.

Her mum was very concerned about her, but she gave her the space she asked for.

Whilst she was in the bedroom, with her door locked, she texted Pilani.

[Hey, my love,
I am in deep trouble. I told my mum about our engagement, and she started yelling at me, saying all sorts. She is more worried about what my dad is going to do. I am really scared of him and don't know what he will do when he gets to find out. What do you think I should do?]

[Okay, listen to me, just stay in your room for now if you have to. You know I'm at work right now. I'll call you as soon as I finish.

Take care, my love,
Love you xxx]
[Love you too xxx]

As soon as Pilani finished work, he contacted Sindi straight away on her mobile phone and suggested the unexpected. He suggested that Sindi run away from home to live with him. He knew that if her father were to find out about their secret engagement, he would make him pay a lot of money for Sindi's bride price.

At this point, Sindi was prepared to sacrifice anything to be with Pilani, including breaking her relationship with her family, especially her mother, whom she cared for dearly.

Sindi carefully planned for her getaway, and she waited for the perfect moment when she was left alone at home. Her parents had gone out to visit relatives, and Sindi took this moment to run away from home to be with the love of her life, Pilani. She packed as many bags as she could carry and she left a note for her mother that read:–

Dear Mum,

I know this note will come as a shock to you. I am writing to let you know that I have decided to leave home and be with the love of my life (you know who). I am very sorry that I have not been the perfect daughter you wanted me to be, and I know I have disappointed you immensely. You raised me well, but Mum, I am now 20 years old, and I can make my own decisions. I know what I want, and I just want to let you know that I love you and Dad dearly. I would like you to understand that you have not done anything wrong to me to cause me to leave home. This is what I want and have decided to do. I am going with my heart. Please don't look for me or worry about me. I will be in good hands, and I know I will be safe. I promise, Mum, I will be in touch with you as soon as I can.

Love you lots xxx
Sindisiwe

Sindi neatly folded the note and placed it next to their microwave, where she knew her mother would easily spot it.

Sindi's mum was the one who discovered the note, and after reading it, she was inconsolable. She sobbed until her face was smeared with tears.

Thoughts raced through her mind. *What did I do wrong? Where did I go wrong as a mother? What could I have done differently? What am I going to tell her father?*

Her heart was beating so fast; she was heartbroken. She had so much hope in Sindi; she started to imagine all the precious moments they spent together cooking. She was more heartbroken to learn that her daughter had decided to leave home to be with a man she hardly knew. She had to break the news to Sindi's father.

"Dear, could you come to the lounge? I need to speak to you about something," she began.

"Is everything okay? You look like you've been crying. What's the matter?" he asked with a concerned look.

"Sindi has run away." She broke the news.

"She has what? How did you find out? We've literally just come back," he barked at his wife, and spit came out as he spoke.

Sindi's mum was very scared, but she had to remain calm not to escalate the situation.

"She left this note in the kitchen," she said and handed it to him.

He started to read the letter, and a vein immediately popped up on his forehead. This was a sign of tension. He was left speechless. Sindi was his only daughter and last child.

"So what are we going to do?" he asked. "Call the police? Do you know the person? I can imagine you know more than I do. I always listened to you giggling with her in the kitchen. She must have told you whom she was seeing," he said.

Sindi's mum knew her husband was right, but on this occasion, she had to withhold information as she did not know what he would do. She knew if she had informed him that Sindi had introduced him to Pilani, he would be mad at her. The worst thing was that he was a teacher at a school near them, and she did not want Sindi's father to report him to the school. She did not know what to do.

"I think we should give it a few days. I believe she will contact us. She will come home at some point, whe..." she said, but her husband cut her sentence off.

"She better not come back. I'll bre...",

Sindi's mum did not let him finish.

"Darling, please. Children can disappoint their parents. Let's see what happens in a couple of days. I'm sure she will phone or something," she said.

"You see, you are still defending her. This is why she behaved like that. She knew you would defend her. Look at this note – it is addressed to you. Please deal with your daughter, but I will make one thing clear: I don't want to see her back here until the person who is with her has paid full dowry," he said.

"I hear you. Let's hope she is okay first before we think of a dowry, dear," she said.

"I'm done with you and your daughter," he said.

"Can I make you a hot drink, dear?" she offered, making attempts to defuse the tension.

"I'm alright for now, thanks," he said.

The two did not speak to each other for a considerable length of time. But after a couple of days had passed and they had not heard from Sindi, they came to terms with the fact that she was okay where she was and would contact them when she was ready.

CHAPTER FIVE

A family is formed

The first year of marriage for Sindi and Pilani was like a modern-day fairytale. One thing that stood out for Pilani was how happy Sindi made him. No one had a sense of humour like she did; every day was filled with laughter. She had a surprise or two up her sleeve for him most days after he came from work, ensuring that the stresses of his day were washed away. As well as being husband and wife, they were the best of friends.

Another great quality about Sindi was that she was very tidy and creative. She totally transformed Pilani's home and made it look like one you would find in a magazine. It was another reason he looked forward to coming home – to an oasis of calm and beauty. In fact, he soon stopped going for drinks after work with his colleagues for that reason. Of course, they teased him about being smitten with his new wife and life. This did not bother him; being in Sindi's company was all that mattered to him.

The couple spent all their time together, in good weather, resting in their small garden shed, and they added travelling to their list of activities. Pilani spoilt Sindi with a lifestyle she was not accustomed to; sometimes, she thought it was too much, but she was nonetheless grateful. In return, she impressed Pilani with her culinary skills, giving him yet another reason to come home straight from work, especially being the foodie that he was. Her freshly baked breads and hearty soups were out of this world, making him boast to his colleagues about what an amazing cook his wife was. They also got to sample her food; Pilani regularly asked

Sindi to prepare cupcakes and scones for him to take to work and share with his workmates. They, too, raved about how great a cook Sindi was, which made Pilani very proud.

There was one feature of her new life that she had not yet got accustomed to. Since moving in with Pilani, Sindi had noticed something very peculiar about one of their neighbours.

"Hey, Pilani, do you speak with your neighbours?" she asked.

"Not really, I keep myself to myself. Why did you ask?"

"When I am in the garden, I have noticed that there is always someone peeping from the window of the house next door."

"Which side? We have two – one on either side."

"I mean the one on our left."

"Oh, you mean 'Ms Poppy,' as I call her. She's very nosy and stands by her window most of the time, scanning the whole street for something to gossip about. I have learnt to ignore her."

"At least now I know."

At the beginning of their relationship, Pilani had also made it clear that he expected to find Sindi at home at all times when he returned from work. Sindi had not objected to this; after all, she had run away from home for him. She trusted him, and she was very happy to focus solely on their relationship. Sindi literally gave their relationship her all. He also made it clear to Sindi that she should not speak with her family without his permission. This caused a total breakdown in any efforts Sindi intended to make to contact her mother, with whom she was very close. She figured that because Pilani loved her so much, this was coming from a good place. They had each other, so there was no reason to worry about their families, or so Sindi thought. Pilani had also cut ties with his family, especially his father.

To their critics, their relationship would appear to have moved too fast and was a recipe for disaster. One sunny morning, as a newly married wife, Sindi continued to make efforts to impress Pilani by doing different things. One of which was to prepare him a daily fresh, healthy snack pack for work. On this day, something peculiar happened. As she was placing the snack box on the table, she felt a tingling sensation in her stomach.

"Whooh...woooh..." were the weird sounds she made whilst she quickly rushed to the bathroom.

"Are you okay, Sindi?" Pilani asked and followed her to the bathroom. He stood by the bathroom door, and all he heard were sounds like she was vomiting.

"Can I open the door, Sindi? Are you being sick?" he asked.

He heard Sindi flushing the toilet.

She washed her hands, rinsed her mouth and opened the bathroom door.

"Whoa, I don't know what that was. I just felt sick. Really horrible feeling," she said.

"Did you eat anything that upset your tummy?" he asked.

"I just had a cup of tea, that's all. I should be alright. Don't worry about me; otherwise, you will be late for work," she answered.

"Okay, hon, I'm off. Send me a text and let me know how you get on. If I need to take some time off, I'll do that," Pilani said.

"Okay, dear, have a great day. I will keep you posted about how I feel," Sindi said.

This experience left Sindi shaken. But a thought quickly entered her mind. *Could I be pregnant?*

Just to be certain, Sindi decided to freshen up quickly and go to the chemist to buy a pregnancy test kit, despite Pilani making it clear to her not to leave the house without informing him.

When she got home, she quickly took the test, and the results shocked her. There were two clear lines on the test strip to indicate that she was pregnant. She immediately slumped to the bathroom floor in disbelief. She did not expect this early on in their marriage; besides, they had not really discussed any plans to start a family. Her feelings started to race; she didn't know whether to text Pilani instantly or wait for him to come back home and then tell him.

Meanwhile, Pilani had sent her a few texts to find out how she was feeling since her health scare earlier in the day.

[Hey Si, how are you feeling now? Any more vomiting?]
[I'm feeling much better, thanks. Thank goodness, I haven't vomited since that time. Don't worry about me; I'm doing fine. See you soon. Love you xxx]
[Love you too xxx]

As always, Sindi was a lady with many surprises up her sleeve, and this day was no different. She, therefore, planned for this special announcement carefully. Throughout the day, she had spent time running around getting special ingredients to make her dish. She knew how much Pilani adored her spicy chicken stew with jollof rice. She topped this by adding spicy dumplings to the meal.

Nearer to the time Pilani usually came home, she had quickly had a hot bath and wore a lovely flowy light blue dress to maintain her usual smart appearance.

When Pilani arrived, the first thing he noticed was a beautiful aroma that filled their kitchen. He hugged Sindi as he always did when he came back home and when leaving.

"Yum, hey, darling, what's that beautiful aromatic smell coming from the kitchen? I can't wait to get this suit off and just dig in," Pilani said.

"I'll prepare the table. Come and join me when you're ready."

"I'll be down in ten."

When Pilani returned to the lounge, he gave Sindi another compliment. "You never cease to amaze me; you're some special lady," he said.

"Thank you, dear," she responded. "I made some dumplings; I hope you like them."

"Like you could ever prepare anything I don't enjoy, come on," he said, sharing a joke with Sindi.

Sindi waited for Pilani to enjoy his food without interrupting him. She planned to tell him about the pregnancy towards the end of their meal.

When Pilani swallowed his last dumpling and placed his cutlery on the table, Sindi found this a perfect timing to break the news.

"Hon, I've got some rather exciting news to share with you…" Sindi began.

"Really? Give it to me; I'm ready," he said excitedly, but his heart had started to beat faster than normal.

"Depends on how you will take it."

"That's a bit scary; I can't keep holding my breath. Please just tell me now. The suspense is killing me; I can't wait a minute longer. What's the news? Come on, tell me!" Pilani asked.

"I'm pregnant," Sindi said.

"You're what? Pregnant? Is this a joke or what?" Pilani exclaimed, laughing nervously.

"I'm actually being deadly serious; I'm pregnant with our first child. I hope it's great news for you, too?"

"Are you kidding me? I'm ecstatic! Hooray! I'm going to be a father! Wow! Sindi, we are going to be parents. No wonder my upper eyelid has been twitching all day. I'm so happy. I can't wait to share the news with my mates tomorrow. This is the best news; you've literally made my day. Any more dumplings? My appetite has just increased," Pilani said excitedly.

"I'm glad you are happy. Of course – I left a few dumplings in the oven," Sindi said.

Pilani immediately stood up, lifted Sindi and swung her around in joy.

"Careful, you don't want to make me throw up all that food I just ate!" Sindi said jokingly.

For the first time, Pilani cleared the table after their meal, which really surprised Sindi. From that day on, he was a different man. He started to help Sindi more with the household chores. She felt loved and supported.

As her baby bump grew, they both started to feel anxious about becoming first-time parents. Excitedly, they decided to go together for Sindi's six-month antenatal scan check-up, and they requested that their doctor reveal the gender of their baby.

On the day, they were both nervous, and from their previous discussions, it was clear that Pilani preferred a son as their first child, and Sindi preferred a daughter.

It was time for the doctor to reveal the gender, and he said to them, "It's a boy! Is this what you were both expecting?" he asked.

"He is happy; he wanted a boy, and I wanted a daughter to take my name after."

"Yessss!" Pilani pumped his fist in excitement. "I'm going to have a mini-me!"

"Have you thought of any names yet?" the doctor asked.

"My mum once told me that she would have named me Tembani if my father had not overpowered her. So I will name him Tembani, which means 'We have hope,'" Pilani said, smiling.

"That is such a beautiful name, and if this baby had turned out to be a girl, are there any names you had in mind?"

"Thandiwe or Thandi, meaning 'The loved one.'" Sindi responded fast, suggesting that if they ever had a daughter, she would undoubtedly name her this.

"Amazing names. Who knows, one day, you may also be blessed with a daughter. I wish both of you all the best," the doctor said.

"Thanks, Doc," they both said at the same time.

"No worries. Sindi, I'll see you at your next appointment," the doctor said as the two left the clinic.

CHAPTER SIX

Tembani is born

The birth of their son brought so much joy to the couple. They stuck to their promise and named him Tembani (Temba for short). Pilani took paternity leave to help Sindi out with the baby. Tembani had brought an even closer bond to the couple.

Pilani was a hands-on father; he cuddled Tembani whilst Sindi attended to the household chores. He put Tembani in his buggy and spent quality time with him at the park and shops. He made sure all his colleagues knew that he had become a new father.

Sindi and Pilani appeared like a perfect couple. However, some issues seemed to go on unaddressed. The absence of their parents or even friends coming to visit them was one issue. It seemed that everything operated only around them and their new baby. Neither of them had informed their parents of the pregnancy or, most importantly, the birth of their son. Sindi did not dare bring this topic up as she was sceptical of how Pilani would react. She also had no means of communicating with her family as Pilani managed her phone credit and checked her call log every now and again. As a young parent and wife, she thought this was LOVE.

She did not see the *'red flags'* of her husband's controlling behaviour. Pilani would ask Sindi to write the list of things she required for their baby, and he would buy everything she needed. Sindi was not allowed to leave their house without Pilani's approval. He did all he could to prevent Sindi from meeting friends or her family. On moving in together, the first thing he did was buy her a new SIM card and destroy her old one. Pilani knew it would be hard for Sindi to remember all her family's mobile numbers.

The only time Sindi enjoyed fresh air was when she sat out in their small garden shed. Tembani's cognitive behavioural development was that which was expected of him at his stage of childhood. He seemed to learn things fast, and Pilani would look at his son and feel proud. Tembani was spoilt rotten by his parents; they got him a lot of toys, more than he needed. He was a happy child and always wore a smile on his face.

Pilani had added another reason to run home after work, not just to spend time with Sindi but to spend quality time with his son. Pilani had developed a new routine when he came home after work. He would always lift his son up and give him a warm cuddle and a little tickle, which made Tembani very happy. Even at a young age, he looked forward to his father coming home, and it didn't take him long to start calling him "Daddy."

Sindi would always say to Tembani jokingly, "You cheeky little fella, you spend more time with me, and you still can't say 'Mummy.' How dare you?"

"Is someone jealous?"

"Of course not," she replied as she rolled her eyes.

The couple adapted well to their new routine as new parents. However, when Tembani was two and a half years old, Sindi dropped a bombshell that Pilani did not see coming.

CHAPTER SEVEN

A surprise goes wrong

Everything seemed to be going very well for the couple. Tembani had added some spice to their love life. However, one day, Sindi noticed she could not stand the smell of eggs as she was making their egg salad. This feeling was familiar, like when she was pregnant with Tembani.

This is ridiculous; I always like egg salad. Today, I am finding it smelly, yuk! Sindi thought, but decided not to share her thoughts with her husband.

It was not only the smell of eggs that she had started to hate, but the smell of her favourite perfume, too.

What is going on? Why do I hate the smells of all the things that I usually like? Goodness me, could I be pregnant again? I hope not. Pilani would not be happy with me this time, she thought.

These emotions went on for some time, and Sindi could not take the torture of these emotions any longer. She was becoming easily irritable for no apparent reason, and Pilani had noticed this behaviour in her.

One day, as Pilani returned from work, as usual, he greeted her with a kiss before he went to pick up Tembani.

"Hey, Si, how was your day today? Has Temba been behaving?"

"Yep. Will you place your jacket properly behind the door, please, before lifting Temba up?"

"Hey, we're not in a good mood today, are we?"

"Please, I just gave you a simple instruction."

"Okay, Ma'am," Pilani joked.

Sindi realised she could not go on feeling like that for much longer, and she asked Pilani something she had not done since they got together.

"Pilani, can I have £10, please? I need to get something from the chemist. I hope you don't mind if I leave you with Tembani for a bit. I just need to pop out quickly."

"What do you need from there? Are you okay? You could have asked me to get whatever you need on my way from work."

"Well, it's something personal."

"What do you mean personal? From me? Hmmm...okay. Please be quick; you know I've never babysat."

"Won't be long."

Sindi put on her jacket and left the house.

She bought two pregnancy test kits just to be sure and rushed back home. As soon as she entered, Pilani was waiting for her by the door, carrying Tembani in his arms.

"Did you get what you wanted?"

"Yes, thanks." She rushed to walk past him as she did not want Pilani to see what she had bought.

"Sindi! What did you get from the chemist?" He asked with a razor-sharp tone.

Sindi was a bit shaken by this; she had never heard Pilani speak to her that way.

"Nothing of importance. I'll tell you in a bit," she said.

"You'd better," he said.

She was familiar with the routine of taking this test. This was a no-brainer; she was pregnant for the second time, and Tembani was only two and a half years old. She was unsure of how to break the news to her husband again. She had no option but to inform Pilani about her unexpected pregnancy again.

"Darling, can we sit down and have a chat?" Sindi said.

"What now? You're not pregnant again, are you?"

"And if I am?"

"Well, I'd say that is a bit careless from your end because we were just getting comfortable with our parenting skills with our son, and now you are adding another one?"

Sindi started to cry.

"What's the matter?"

"You speak like everything is my fault. I forgot to take my contraception pill once; I am sorry."

"No need to apologise. It is what it is now. But I will be honest with you: I was not ready for another child this early on, considering that Tembani is still a baby, and we're still potty training him."

"I'm so sorry," Sindi apologised again.

This time, Pilani gave her a hug. He then immediately turned his back to her and started to address Tembani. "Tembani, come here, Son, listen to me. You are going to be a big brother soon, hey!" He tickled his cheeks. "Your mother just couldn't wait a few more years to give you a baby sister or brother. What do you think, big boy? What would you prefer?" he joked with Tembani.

Tembani just giggled from the tickling from his father. He didn't understand what was going on between his parents.

"Seriously, Pilani? I find that very annoying and childish. Grow up."

"Come on, Sindi, where is your sense of humour? I'm just joking. I think you're being overly sensitive. Maybe the hormones are playing tricks on you, don't you think? Sorry if I crossed the line."

"Maybe your jokes aren't just funny, let's just say that," Sindi said solemnly.

"I'm so sorry, darling," he said, and kissed her on the cheek.

The revelation of Sindi's second pregnancy brought a different side to Pilani that she had not seen up to this point in their relationship, and more was still to come.

CHAPTER EIGHT
A trigger that changes their lives forever

Since Sindi had moved in with Pilani, he had always maintained the same routine of coming home at almost exactly the same time every day after work, except when he had a meeting or sports day. However, after announcing her second pregnancy to him, she started to notice a change in his behaviour. He began to come home later than usual. At times, his tie would be slightly pulled lower from his neck, and the top of his shirt button undone.

"What's up with this new look?" she asked.

"What do you mean? Which look?"

"This look," she said, pointing her finger at him and moving it up and down. "You're just looking a bit rough lately. Look at your tie, and what is it about the overgrown beard? It's unlike you. You look like you've just come out of a washing machine."

"It's a bit warm out there, darling; I thought I would just let my neck breathe some fresh air. Satisfied?"

"And the beard? You're also blaming that on the heat? Please, have a shave; you look ridiculous right now. I'm sure your colleagues at work think you're losing your plot."

"Yes, Ma'am," he answered and gave a salute gesture.

Nine months went by so fast, and the couple welcomed another baby boy, naming him Sipho, which means 'A gift.' They perceived having two sons to be a blessing. As Tembani was now three, it was clear, even from this young age, that he had a caring side to him. It showed in the way he

41

behaved towards his little brother. He always asked his mum if he could hold baby Sipho whenever he saw her busy in the house and would want to help out.

He's such a caring young man, Sindi always thought to herself.

Each time Tembani asked Sindi to hold his brother in his arms, she would ask him to sit down on the sofa. She would place Sipho gently on his lap before adding one or two cushions on either side of him to ensure that he was secure, comfortable and safe.

"You're a big boy now, Tembani. Check you out! You can hold your brother safely, and look; he's smiling at you!" Sindi would praise him.

This would make Tembani very happy. He would grin broadly. He enjoyed being called a 'big boy.'

Apart from enjoying moments when he could hold his brother in his arms, he also always looked forward to his father coming home from work to play football with him in their small garden. Pilani always found a bit of time to play football with his son in their garden. He would also race him around their yard, and Tembani absolutely loved this. Sindi would watch them adoringly through the kitchen window, and she admired their growing father and son bond.

The couple continued to get on with their lives smoothly without any involvement of their families. At the age of five, Tembani started junior school, and Sipho was at preschool. Sindi had developed a new routine. On every school day, she would make sure she prepared the meals before going on the school run. She also did not want her husband to come back home from work and not find his food prepared.

When Tembani started school, his first teacher, Miss Chioma, told Sindi that he was such a brilliant student and a fast learner compared to other children of his age group. She was also amazed that at the age of five, he could count numbers up to one hundred, as not all her students were able to do this.

One day, when she came to pick him up after school, Miss Chioma said to Sindi, "Good afternoon, Sindi. I just wanted to tell you again that Tembani is such a joy to teach. He is such a smart kid. He is very advanced for his age. Were you or his father like that when you were younger?" she asked.

"His father is a teacher; I guess he takes after him."

"You don't need to be a teacher to be smart."

"Hmmm.... Okay, thanks for letting me know."

"One more thing, he likes tidying up things, which is so unusual for children of his age group. He seems very structured and likes to follow a certain routine."

Sindi suddenly felt ashamed that she had not even completed her education, but she did not want to embarrass herself in front of her son's teacher.

"I guess the tidying bit is definitely from me," she admitted. "I like routine, and I am very particular about where I place things. I don't like it when people move things around from where I would have placed them," Sindi said with a smile.

"Where does your husband teach?" Miss Chioma asked.

"Bryanston Secondary School."

"That's a very good school, very reputable for great grades. Anyways, see you tomorrow," she said.

"Bye, Miss Chioma."

Tembani's mum seems like she has autistic traits. I wonder if she is aware of this, Miss Chioma thought as Sindi walked away.

After picking up Tembani, Sindi always rushed to pick up Sipho from his preschool before hurrying back home. She had a set time given by Pilani to get home. This didn't allow time to get to know other parents or socialise with them as she was always in a rush.

On this day, when Pilani came back home from work, Tembani was eagerly waiting for him to tell him what Miss Chioma had said about him. As soon as Pilani entered through the door, Tembani ran, and his father lifted him up.

"Hello, Son, you seem so excited today. Did you get a star?"

"Dad, Dad, my teacher said I was very good at school, and Mum said I get this from you. Is this true, Dad?"

"I guess if your mum said so, then it is correct. What do you think, Son? Do you think Daddy is smart? Hey?" Pilani asked as he started to tickle him, making Tembani giggle.

"Dad, when I grow up, I want to be a maths teacher like you," Tembani said with excitement.

Unknowingly to the little boy, this was an immediate trigger for Pilani that no one saw coming. He had been keeping a big, dark secret from his family all this while.

One day, as they sat around the dinner table having a snack, an unexpected event happened that would change their relationship forever. Sindi had noticed that her children had finished eating, and it was nearly bedtime.

"Boys, it's eight o'clock. Come on, it's bedtime. You're going to school tomorrow. Quick, quick, boys, Let's go upstairs. Brush your teeth and put on your PJs," she said.

She helped Sipho to put on his pyjamas before tucking him into bed. Tembani had already hopped into his bed and waited for his mum to read them a short bedtime story. After her children had drifted off to sleep, Sindi returned to join Pilani in the lounge.

When she got back, Pilani had already left the table and gone to their bedroom. A little baffled, Sindi followed him to their bedroom.

"Are you alright, dear? I was just getting the children to bed. I thought I would find you in the lounge."

"Why did you do that?" Pilani asked.

"Do what? What are you talking about?"

"Just standing up and taking the children to bed before we had finished eating and without excusing yourself?"

"I beg your pardon? I should excuse myself in my own house? And apologise for taking our children to bed? Are you kidding me?" Sindi responded. She was not happy with Pilani.

"It is called having table manners, dear."

"You're just looking for trouble with me, aren't you? And this is not right."

"Can you sit down on the bed, please? Don't stand over me when you're talking."

"Okay," Sindi said, sitting on the edge of the bed. "Is everything alright? You just seem angry for some reason."

"Sindi, I have something to tell you that I have been bottling inside for some time." Pilani spoke in a flat and forlorn tone.

She sat up straight and looked in his direction.

"I hope everything is alright."

"Not really. Sindi, I can't take this anymore." Pilani seemed very fidgety, as if agitated.

"Take what? What's happened?"

"I'm very sorry to tell you that I am not happy at work, and I have tried to keep this from you for a long time. To be honest with you, I never even had the passion to become a teacher. When Tembani said he wants to become a teacher like me when he grows up, this just triggered my childhood emotions of my father forcing me to become a teacher. I did not have a passion for teaching, and now my son wants to become like me. But who am I? I don't know myself, and I will not allow my son to become the person I hate. What I hate is 'me.' I want my son to be happy and choose what *he* wants to become and not to be like me. I need to figure out who I am before I can allow my son to become what I hate."

Sindi's mouth fell open in disbelief. "But...but you did not ask him to become a teacher. He just wants to follow in your footsteps."

"They are not *my* footsteps, Sindi! Why don't you understand that? What I am is not ME! This is my father's dream and not mine. He forced me to be a teacher, and that was not my dream. My dream was to become a gamer."

Sindi had not seen this coming and had not picked up any signs that her husband was unhappy in his job.

"How did your father force you to become a teacher?" Inwardly, she was thinking, *What is going on with my husband?* "Pilani, you are so good at your job. What happened? Did someone upset you at work or something? Maybe what you need is to take some time to think over this, don't you think?" she responded calmly.

"There is nothing to think about, okay? I have made up my mind. I don't like the job, period! I am sick and tired of people telling me what is good and what is not good for me without considering my feelings, my thoughts or my choices or asking me what I think is good for me! Alright?" Pilani spoke angrily.

"I don't get this; you were triggered by your son wanting to be like you? And this upset you to this extent?"

"Sindi, you're clearly not paying attention to what I am telling you. If my father had not forced me to be a teacher, I would not have been one in the first place. Does that make sense to you? Now my son wants to be like me! The question is, Who is me? Huh? Who is Pilani? I don't know who I am! And I will not allow my son to follow in my footsteps because they're not mine. I want him to be Tembani and not me!!! I need to figure out who I am first. Right now, all I know is I am just an illusion of someone else's dream. Now my son wants to become everything that I hate, and I don't want to hate my son for becoming what I hate in me."

Sindi wished the ground would just swallow her whole. She felt perplexed. She didn't know what to say or do.

"These are very strong words and deep feelings of pain, Pilani. Is it me? Did I do anything to upset you? Or am I in a dreamland right now?" Sindi asked, looking very confused.

"Sindi, it's not all about you, do you hear me? Stop asking me too many questions. This is actually irritating me, and I don't have time for that kind of chat right now!" Pilani continued to speak angrily.

"Stop yelling at me! Do you understand that this is the first time you've told me about this? And I am kind of struggling to absorb everything said just now. I'm actually as confused about you as you're about yourself. Please don't be angry with me. I want to understand where you are coming from, and this may take some time. Did I hear you say you wanted to become a gamer?"

"That is correct. That's what I wanted to do."

"A gamer? And waste your maths talent?"

"What do you know about being a gamer, and who told you gamers don't need a maths talent? You don't want me to insult your intelligence. So don't make me go there."

"Just because I didn't complete my education doesn't mean I don't know anything about gaming. I actually feel insulted by your remark. Calm down, please. So was maths the only reason your father wanted you to become a teacher?"

"In his reasoning, he thought being a gamer was a waste of time and would not make as much money as being a teacher. He is of the old generation and does not want to shift from that mindset. Besides, he did not even give me a chance to tell him that my intention was to use my talent to develop my own video games, but that is all a dream now. I want my son to have a choice of his own and to have a voice that I never had." Pilani paused for a bit.

"I will do whatever it takes to prevent my son from going through what I went through. You know what, Sindi? Even talking to you right now aggravates the anger that was lying dormant within me. In fact, I don't wish to speak to you about my father anymore or my son. I have come to the conclusion that I will have nothing to do with him anymore! He will never see me or his grandchildren, I can tell you that. Parents are known for disowning their children, but in my case, I am disowning my own father for ruining my life. He is a nasty and selfish man who does not want to change old ways," he said.

"I guess, as a parent, he thought he was doing this for your own good." Sindi spoke slowly so as not to upset her husband further.

Pilani was not in the right mood to entertain any explanation that would justify his father's behaviour.

"My own good? Seriously, Sindi? To force me to do what I didn't want to do? And you say that was for my own good? You want to know something else about him? When I was young and at school, even if I got eighty percent on an exam, he would beat the hell out of me, telling me that I wasn't good enough and needed to study more. One other thing you need to know, my father never hugged us. I mean, my siblings and I. His explanation was that we would get too close to him and disrespect him in the end, so he always showed us his tough side and not the softer side of him. Which, if you asked me now, I still don't know that side of him," he said.

"What? I'm confused about the first part. You were beaten up for getting eighty percent? Surely this can't be right. He really expected you to get 100 percent marks in everything? That was a bit extreme. And hugging his children? I don't get where the disrespect would come from. Is hugging your children not a sign of love? It's a difficult one. I am really sorry that this is what you had to go through."

This was the first time Sindi was hearing this about her husband and his relationship with his father.

"Do you now see what I mean? That is what makes me angry. For all my life, I grew up believing I was a failure and not good enough at anything other than what I was told I should believe I am good at. Never in all my childhood did I hear my father say to me, 'Well done, my son' or 'I am proud of you.' All I ever heard him say was bragging about his family being very educated people and that we had to be the same. He always said, 'Why don't you be like Aunty this or Uncle So-and-so, who are lawyers or some professor somewhere?'

"It was always what he thought was right for us, and we had no voice to say what we wanted. With him, it was always his way or no way, and he was 'always right.' My father cared more about his reputation than keeping us and Mum happy. Now look! I am stuck with a job I hate for the rest of my life. I just can't go on pretending anymore. I just can't," Pilani said.

"You're still young, Pilani. You still have the chance to do what you wanted. Can I ask you something? When all this was happening, what was your mum's thoughts?"

"Mum could never defend us. She was not allowed to oppose my father. In my culture, a wife must follow the lead of her husband. The man is the head of the household, and to oppose him is disrespectful," Pilani said.

"Really? Even if what he says is wrong? I see. I hope you don't believe that..." Sindi murmured.

Pilani gave her a stern look but did not respond to her last comment.

"You asked me if I could still be a gamer," he continued. "I want to ask you a question. Have you ever dealt with trauma, and do you know what it is? If not, I would appreciate you not making suggestions. You do not understand what I am going through and how long I have been dealing with it, suggesting that I can just brush all my feelings aside and switch easily to something else."

"I am sorry for what I said, and you're right; it only takes the person affected to know exactly how they feel in themselves. I can imagine this must have been very tough for you," Sindi empathised.

"In fact, I felt so powerless as a child. Communication was parent to child and not child to parent."

"I would not want us to bring up our children like that," Sindi said bravely.

"Do you recall the way he treated you when I introduced you to him? And how unwelcome you felt, so we left earlier than we had planned. He also used to repeatedly say this annoying statement to us: 'Don't make me a laughing stock,' putting his family's opinions over us. One other thing you need to know is that on that day I introduced you to him, he asked me if I was right in my senses to choose you as a wife because of your educational background and the children thing he said to you. Do you remember that?" Pilani asked.

"I am so appalled."

After this revelation, without warning, Pilani just stood up from their bed. "I'm going out," he declared.

"Where are you going?" Sindi asked. She was surprised that her husband was just leaving their house at night without telling her where he was going.

"I need to get some fresh air outside."

"Have you even checked what time it is? It's nearly nine o'clock, and you are working tomorrow. Come on, get your act together. It is not safe out there at this time."

"Sindi, at this point, I really don't care, okay?"

Pilani left the room and slammed the door behind him. Sindi was left confused and speechless as this was the first time her husband had behaved in this way.

In a state of confusion, she stood up and went back to their lounge. She started to tidy up. She washed up the dishes and watched television programmes she had never watched before. She waited for her husband to return home. In her mind, he was just having a bad moment and was going for a walk to clear his mind.

Pilani returned home very late and smelt strongly of alcohol. This was the first time in the time they had been together that he had pulled a stunt like this. Sindi watched in disbelief as her husband opened the door and stumbled all over the place. He then just threw himself on the sofa next to where she was sitting. All she could do was help him to remove his shoes so he could be comfortable. She did not ask him any questions, as it was not a good idea to start any meaningful conversations with him in this state.

She left him to sleep on the sofa, but she remembered to put her alarm on to remind herself to wake him up to go to work the following morning at his usual time.

Sindi was restless all night. She hardly slept, thinking of what had just happened. To her, this was just a nightmare she would wake up from. They were sleeping in separate rooms for the first time since they had lived together: Sindi alone in their bedroom and Pilani on the sofa. A thought came to her that she had observed a change in her husband when she announced her second pregnancy. His behaviour was no longer consistent, and he had started to come home late. Now, things had started to unravel in front of her eyes.

A question haunted her thoughts.

Is this the first time he has drunk alcohol?

Sadly for Sindi, this was just the beginning of a new chapter of her life.

CHAPTER NINE

Sindi makes a brave decision

From that day on, their relationship with each other steadily deteriorated. Pilani drank even more alcohol, spent less time at home and was constantly ill-tempered. It took a while for Sindi to accept that their relationship had changed. The fairytale romance she had once dreamt of had disappeared. She started to notice too that his behaviour towards their children had changed, something she excused in him for some time, believing he was going to change.

Pilani frequently raised his voice whenever he was speaking to her and their young children without any good reason. Tembani started to be scared of his father, and each time he came back home from work, Tembani would avoid him and go to the bedroom he shared with his brother, where he would pretend to be busy. He stopped running towards his father but ran away from him.

One day, after he came back home from work, Pilani found Tembani talking to his mum in the kitchen.

He asked him fiercely, "What are you doing in here? Are you a mummy's boy? Have you finished your homework? Come on, go to your bedroom now and do your homework. Stop hanging around the kitchen with women and behave like a man," Pilani snapped.

"Sipho, I am going upstairs to do my homework. Are you coming?" Tembani was very protective of his younger brother and did not want to leave him in trouble with his father.

"Okay," Sipho said and followed his brother upstairs.

When they got to their bedroom, Tembani started to teach his brother how to count numbers using his fingers. He sang an alphabet song to help him remember the alphabet letters. Sipho loved this.

After Tembani completed his own homework, he was constantly checking at the door handle, fearing that his father would come and shout at him. He had become so fearful of him. He knew if he caught him not doing his schoolwork, he would give him a beating.

It had become a usual norm that every night, both his and his younger brother's sleep was disturbed by the constant row of their parents from the next room. At times, they would hear banging sounds as though a fight was taking place. The two brothers would just stay in their beds and would not say a word but just listen, powerless.

In the mornings, Sindi would always put on a bright face and sometimes wear heavy make-up to cover bruises from beatings. She never wanted her children to see pain or worry in her expression.

At eight years old, Tembani was at a stage where he could understand that his home environment had become very unhappy. All he witnessed was constant arguments between his parents and, at times, even physical altercations. He became very unhappy and withdrawn. Even though Sindi tried hard to protect her children from these feelings, she noticed that they were no longer spending time around their father. He stopped playing football with them in their garden and always gave them an excuse that he was too tired from work to play games with them as he used to.

One day, as Sindi picked Tembani up from his year four class, his teacher, Mr Hardy, asked to speak with her in private.

"Hello there, Tembani's mum. I wanted to speak to you privately about Tembani. I have noticed lately that he has been sleeping a lot in my classes, and it is very unusual for him to do this. Is he going to bed late at home?"

"Not that I know of. But I will keep an eye on this. Thanks for letting me know." Sindi was not comfortable discussing her home life with Mr Hardy.

"He is usually a very bubbly boy, and I have noticed that recently, he seems to be quite withdrawn and not mixing with other children as much as he used to. I don't mean to make you worry too much, but his performance in class has also gone down significantly, and his concentration has become very poor. Tembani is a very bright boy, and I just thought it's good I share this information with you so that we can work together to find out what could be the cause of this and do something to help him."

"Thank you for letting me know, Mr Hardy. I will keep an eye on him if he is staying awake at night. Please let me know from your end if this behaviour continues."

"Certainly, I will update you and thank you for your time."

"You're welcome."

Sindi was so heartbroken to hear this report about her son. Deep down, she knew that her home environment was no longer a happy one for her and her children, but she didn't know that it was having such a negative impact on her eldest son at school.

When Pilani came home, Sindi did not get the chance to discuss Mr Hardy's concerns about Tembani with him because he was, as always, intoxicated with alcohol. This behaviour from Pilani had become the norm for the couple, and their relationship was strained.

Pilani's abuse towards his wife increased. He snapped at her at any given opportunity, did not pay attention to their two children and stopped communicating with Sindi respectfully, which made her very sad. Sindi was a tough cookie, and she made all efforts to endure the abuse from her husband with optimism that surely, one day, things would change for the better. She loved her husband and would do anything to support him through this difficult time he was going through, so she thought. Her love for Pilani was so great, and this gave her the utmost hope.

It was during this challenging period of their relationship that Sindi found out she was expecting their third child. From an external point of view, it was not an ideal situation to add another child to their already strained relationship. However, from Sindi's perspective, having another child could be a good reason for her husband to have a change of heart regarding their relationship. She remained optimistic. She knew this would be her last child as she always hoped to have three children in her lifetime. But yet again, she had to figure out the best way to break this news to Pilani.

A few weeks went by, and Sindi was sceptical of how she would break this news to her husband. What made her situation more difficult was the fact that Pilani always came home drunk, and she knew how hard it was to have a meaningful conversation with him when he was under the influence of alcohol. But Sindi knew she had to break the news at some point. Time was moving on, and she did not want Pilani to see the growing bump before she informed him.

One night, she braved herself to inform her husband. She decided to reveal her pregnancy on this particular night because Pilani seemed more sober than usual. She initiated the conversation hesitantly, but she had to speak to him before he fell asleep.

"Hey, hon, can I talk to you about something please, before you go to sleep?"

"What about, Sindi?" he asked. "At this time? Come on! It better be something sensible."

Sindi's heart started to beat at a mile a minute. She tried to be in a playful mood and was hiding the pregnancy test behind her back.

"What are you hiding behind you?"

"Guess first."

"Sindi, I don't have time for all this. I'm tired, and I need to sleep. Are you forgetting I've got work tomorrow?"

Her face instantly dropped in disappointment, but she remained hopeful that Pilani's mood would soon lift when he saw the surprise she was hiding. She slowly took out the test from behind her and waved it to him in style.

"Ta-da! Look what I have!",

She waved the pregnancy test towards his face with a huge smile on hers.

"What's that?"

"Can't you see? It's positive, look!" She moved the testing kit closer to his eyes. "Darling, we are expecting our third child."

"Really? Another one? You must be out of your mind! Is this a joke or something? At times, I wonder what goes on inside that head of yours! Another child so soon? Are the two children we have not enough? I think my father was right about you. Listen, if you want peace tonight, just let me sleep, okay?" Pilani fumed.

Sindi felt like a stab in her chest. *'My father was right about you.'* Those words from her husband kept ringing in her head. She felt humiliated and was heartbroken. She wished the floor would swallow her alive. She left the bedroom immediately and went to their bathroom in floods of tears.

What have I done? she asked herself.

After a moment of recuperating, she returned to their bedroom and found out that Pilani had, in actual fact, moved himself towards the edge of their bed. His head was covered with their duvet, and he was facing away from her. The whole night, they never spoke to each other again. It felt like the longest night of her entire life. Their relationship from this day went from bad to worse, not like she had previously hoped.

The news of expecting a third child drove Pilani to drink even more, and this time, in the presence of their young children. Every conversation they had now turned into bouts of arguments. One day, Tembani, who had had enough of his parents' squabbles, reacted to this by crying.

Pilani immediately snapped and shouted at Sindi instead. "Will you stop this boy from crying!"

"What do you mean *this boy*? Are you serious, Pilani? You are referring to our son as 'this boy.' You should be ashamed of yourself. You've taken your frustrations too far, and I will not sit back and watch you take your issues out onto our children. Did you ask him why he is crying?"

"He's making noise, and I can't stand it. I have a headache right now."

"Your headache is caused by your constant drinking and not by Tembani's crying. You're drinking far too much, Pilani. Can't you see how this is affecting us? You need to stop this!"

Sindi was desperate, young and naïve. She didn't know how to deal with her husband's situation. She believed that shouting at him would make him change, and how wrong she was. She only exacerbated his situation.

"Sindi, I said take your son upstairs now! Before I lose it," he warned.

As for Sipho, he was too scared to make a noise, and he just let tears roll silently down his cheeks. He sat on the stairs with his head in his hands, staring at his parents as they yelled at each other.

Sensing danger for her son, Sindi quickly asked Tembani to go to his room.

"Tembani, please go to your room; I'll be with you in a minute."

"Yes, Mum, but will you be okay?"

"Tembani, just do what I have asked you, okay?"

Sipho also stood up from the stairs in fear and followed his brother. When he got to their room, he just hopped into his bed and covered up his head with a blanket, fearing that his father would catch him crying and beat him up.

Sindi immediately follows her two sons to their room.

"Listen, boys, Daddy is not very happy at the moment. He may shout here and there, but you're safe and he loves you, okay? Go to bed now, and Tembani, don't forget to put your alarm on for school tomorrow, okay?" she said.

"Yes, Mum. Are you reading us a story today?" Tembani asked.

"Of course, Son," she answered, but her heart was hurting inside.

Sindi read a short storybook and stayed with her children until they drifted off to sleep. She wanted to make them feel safe.

On a separate occasion, during one of Sindi and Pilani's typical constant rows, Tembani had witnessed what no child should ever see. He watched his father slap his mother across her face for preparing a meal he didn't like, so he snapped.

"Dad, stop! Why are you hitting Mum? You're a monster. I hate you! I hate you!" Tembani hurriedly went to his mother and gave her a tight hug.

Pilani was not in the slightest moved by Tembani's cry for help.

"Are you okay, Mum?"

"Yes, my son, I'm fine," she said as tears rolled down her cheeks.

"Sorry, Mum, I love you."

"I love you too, Son."

Tembani did not know what to do to help his mother, and he started to cry, too.

"Stop crying like a woman! Men don't cry. If you want to grow up a weak man, keep crying," Pilani yelled.

Tembani just looked up at his father. His bulging eyes filled with fear and anger.

"Leave me alone, Dad. Leave me alone! Why are you hurting Mum? I'll call the police on you!"

"Get upstairs now!!! Before I..." Pilani shouted with such a loud voice, spit coming out of his mouth, making Tembani tremble with fear.

Tembani ran quickly to their bedroom and was shaking. He was very scared.

Sipho, who never spoke much, moved towards his brother and hugged him.

"Stop crying, Tembani, stop crying," he said, patting his brother's back.

59

"Okay. Thank you, Sipho."
The two brothers shared a warm hug.

Sindi had sustained a black eye from the slap, and she could not take this anymore. She could not carry on watching her children live in constant fear. She impulsively braved herself up and challenged Pilani on this occasion.

"Will you stop this behaviour now? I am serious. Do you hear me? Your drinking is out of control, and this needs to stop! Look at what you're doing to your children. You're scaring them; they are scared of their own father. Where is the love you had for them? Look at yourself. You look a mess. Look at us. I can't take this anymore. I can't, no! No! Enough is enough. I have had enough, Pilani! Look at you. Are you not affected by the same thing you are asking your son not to do? Do you feel strong now? Can you see what your family has done to you? I will not let you do the same to our children. No way."

Sindi was in floods of tears. Her marriage had just disintegrated in front of her eyes.

Pilani was too drunk to absorb anything Sindi was telling him. He continued to yell at her. "Are you shouting at me, Sindi? I will tell you this once and for all. Don't you ever, EVER tell me how to raise my children. You are my wife, and you only do what I tell you to do, do you hear me? If you EVER tell me again how to raise my son, you will regret it, and I mean that."

As a woman and a mother, Sindi felt defeated and shattered. She glared at Pilani but could not even bring herself to challenge him because he was just not the same man anymore. Her husband's behaviour sent chills of fear down her spine. Clearly, he was no longer the man she had fallen in love with and married. The voice that she was once attracted to was no longer captivating. It now caused her to tremble with fear. She had once adored his height, finding it appealing, but now it intimidated and threatened her. All her dreams of having a fairytale marriage had shattered right in front of her eyes.

Something had absolutely gone wrong. Her husband's behaviour towards her and their children had become unbearable and was a true reflection of how he had described his own father raising him when he was a child.

Day after day, Sindi thought continuously about what to do about her husband's behaviour. She was totally confused; her husband was sadly mirroring his father's behaviour that he condemned. Clearly, history was just repeating itself.

This behaviour from Pilani did not get better as Sindi had hoped. Instead, it escalated from shouting to using physical aggression towards her, and this was continuously witnessed by her two young sons, who were defenceless. Tembani was too young to do anything to help every time he witnessed his father not just shouting at his mother but physically assaulting her. However, out of fear of being beaten by his father, too, he would just move himself and his younger brother to a safe place where they would both curl up and cry themselves to sleep.

When Sindi noticed the impact the abuse was having on her two young sons, she knew it was time to act and do something about it. She could not protect her children, and for her, this was an unforgivable act of her motherhood and parenthood. It was time to face the truth and make a life-changing decision that would have a substantial impact not just on her but on the entire family.

She thought deeply about her decision, and there was no turning back. She had to ask her husband to leave their marital home. Sindi knew this was the hardest decision she could ever make as she had no money because she did not work. But things could not be worse than the life she was living with Pilani. She decided to protect her children and her unborn baby rather than continue to endure the physical and emotional abuse.

One Saturday morning, almost five months after she had disclosed her pregnancy to Pilani, a decision had come to her mind after a lot of deep consideration about her circumstances. Whilst at their dinner table, he had presented himself in one of his drunken episodes, and Sindi seized this moment to break her silence. She gathered courage and boldly confronted her husband.

"Pilani, I can't take this anymore. You shout at me and the children all the time for no apparent reason. You don't even care that you beat me in front of your children. I will not allow you to damage our family any further. I have made my decision, and it is final. I want you to leave the house immediately and get the help you need."

Pilani looked up at her in disdain. "You are asking me to leave? Who do you think you are? The Queen? Where do you expect me to go? Tell me. You have clearly lost your mind. Speak, don't just stare at me. Do you have a place for me to go!!!?" Pilani barked at Sindi.

"I really don't care where you go, Pilani. I've just had enough of your drinking, insensitivity and your abuse. Go and get help. I can't take this anymore; I just can't. Please, leave!" Sindi started to sob and begged her husband to leave their house.

"Are you sure about this?"

"Absolutely."

"What are you going to tell the children, hey? That you asked their father to leave? Okay, tell you what. I will pack all my bags, and I will leave you in peace, if that's what you want," Pilani said.

"Thank you! I would rather they grow up without a father than witness your abuse a minute longer," she responded.

"There is something that you are forgetting, though. Do I need to remind you? Firstly, you don't go to work. How are you going to manage to look after them? Secondly, you relied on me for everything. Thirdly, these are boys. When they are older, they will need their father, and I'm their father no matter what. I hope you will tell them the truth: that *you* asked me to leave! And tell you what? I will not even beg you to let me stay. I am granting you your wish. The house is now yours. Happy? I am leaving, and I hope you will be happy without me. You will NEVER see me again!" Pilani said.

"So be it," Sindi replied.

Pilani hurriedly went into their bedroom, breathing heavily. He started removing all his clothes off the hangers harshly, shoving them into bags and a suitcase, murmuring to himself. When he finished 'packing,' he walked back and forth in their small landing hallway, hastily pressing buttons on his mobile phone. He quickly managed to reserve a room in a bed and breakfast hotel. When the accommodation was confirmed, he rang for a taxi to take him to the hotel.

Sindi, who stood a distance away from Pilani with her arms crossed in front of her, remained in shock, imagining that this could actually mark the end of their fairytale marriage. As soon as the taxi pulled up outside their front yard, Pilani grabbed his belongings and slammed the door behind him. He did not say goodbye to Sindi or the children.

Sindi felt like she had been stabbed in the heart. She just slumped on her knees and broke down. She was in floods of tears. Her emotions were all mixed up; on the one hand, she still loved her husband, but on the other hand, she knew that she had made the right decision: he needed help. In her heart, the most important thing to her at that moment was her safety and that of her children.

When the children woke up the following morning, it was obvious that their father was absent from the house.

"Morning, Mum," Tembani said.

"Good morning, Tembani. How are you this morning?"

"I'm good. Were you crying, Mum? Your eyes are all red, and you don't look happy. What is wrong?" He moved closer to his mother and gave her a hug.

"Nothing, Son, nothing. Should I make you your favourite cereal? Or do you want to make it yourself? You are a big boy now. Come on, let me see you make it. Get the milk from the fridge."

In excitement, Tembani rushed to get the milk and his favourite cereal. He sat with his mum at the table, enjoying his breakfast.

"Mum, where is Dad? He is usually here having his breakfast."

"Tembani, your father has gone away for a while."

"Did he go on a school trip? You know my teacher said we will be going to one soon."

"Okay, Tembani, eat your breakfast whilst I get Sipho up. Otherwise, you will both be late."

"Yes, Mum."

Sindi did not know how to tell him that his father had left home and possibly for good. As she did not know what was going to happen, she decided not to discuss this in-depth with Tembani.

Every day, the children would ask her about the absence of their father. Sindi kept telling them he had decided to take some time away from home but would return soon.

Days turned into weeks, weeks became months, and she still did not tell her sons about their father leaving home. A new, unknown chapter was about to unfold in front of her. She felt scared and alone.

CHAPTER TEN

A new life for Sindi unfolds, and a surprise reunion is on the cards

As any children of their age would do, as time went by, Tembani and Sipho stopped asking about the whereabouts of their father. They were kind of relieved that he was not there because there was no more shouting in the house, and they felt safe with their mum.

The first few weeks of living as a single parent proved to be very challenging for Sindi. The thought of being alone just scared her. She started thinking of things she wouldn't have thought of when Pilani was still at home, and these thoughts haunted her. She started to imagine how she would protect her children if she had a break-in. She became very paranoid, constantly checking that all the doors and windows were locked at all times, and any sound would cause her to jump, especially at night.

However, as the weeks turned into months, Sindi slowly got used to her new single lifestyle. Sipho was also now of school-going age, so Sindi had become accustomed to waking both boys up in the mornings and preparing breakfast for them. She always prepared fresh scones and cupcakes for them to take to school, as she could not afford to pay for their school dinners. Her children loved her cooking and baking, just like their father did.

Sindi was now financially dependent mainly on state benefits for all of her family's upkeep. However, the money she was receiving was not enough for her and the children. Watching them go to school in torn uniforms and shabby, ill-fitting shoes really broke her heart. What comforted her was seeing them playing with each other and wearing happy smiles all the time despite their circumstances.

Sindi had no one to vent her problems to. She had no friends and had distanced herself from her family when everything was going well within her marriage. She only spoke to her neighbours sporadically when they passed by her house, but she never discussed her personal issues with them.

As the weeks had turned into months, the fear and isolation nearly consumed her. The one thing that saved her from totally losing her mind was her children. She knew she had to be strong for them and would do anything to make them happy and give them a better life.

Her biggest challenge yet to come was that of expecting her third child as a single parent. She was due to give birth in a month, and she was becoming very desperate for help. She knew she needed some extra support as she was finding it exhausting doing everything by herself whilst heavily pregnant.

One night, when the children were in bed, Sindi was sitting at the dining table, thinking and worrying about all that was to come. It was in these moments, alone, without the boys to distract her, that she felt on the brink of despair. No matter how many theories she came up with, she could not see any possible way she would be able to look after her two sons and a newborn all by herself. There was only one option that stood out in her mind.

I need to reach out to Mum. But I don't know if she will forgive me for not being there for all these years.

Sindi had not spoken to her family for many years. Pilani had given her an order that he did not want her family or his own around.

How could I be so dumb to let a man break my ties with my entire family? All the wishy-washy things he told me – where is he now? Now I'm all alone and have no one to turn to.

She thought of this and just shook her head in disbelief at how her life had transformed from good to bad.

One morning, she woke up and decided to swallow her pride and reach out to her mother. This was a very difficult decision for Sindi to make. She had not seen her family for a very long time. Later that day, when she reached her parents' door, she became hesitant and felt scared. It was as though she had not lived there before.

Sindi gathered courage, and she knocked on the door gently. She was not aware who would be home at the time. Fortunately, her mother opened the door, and when she saw Sindi heavily pregnant, she just broke down. It was a case of mixed emotions, tears of joy and sadness. She was obviously happy to see her daughter after such a long time, but also a bit disappointed that Sindi had spent so long without communicating with them. But as she was always a caring mother, she was pleased to see her daughter looking well. She asked her to come into the house and make herself comfortable.

"Can I offer you something to drink? What would you like? A hot or cold drink?" Sindi's mum asked.

"A cold drink would do, Mum, thanks."

She stood up and took a chilled drink from the fridge for Sindi.

"So, how have things been? It's been a while. So, what brought you here today? And you look so sad. What is the matter?"

"Well, first of all, I would like to say I am very, very sorry, Mum, for not coming home to see you for this while. I will not give any excuses, and I allowed myself to be in this situation I am in. And I ask for your forgiveness."

"Sindi, home is home. You will always be welcome back here."

"I hope you are all okay."

"Certainly, everyone is fine, dear. You came alone. I was expecting to see little ones with you. I can see you have a bun in the oven! Is this your first one?"

"No, Mum. In fact, I am expecting our third one."

"Oh really? That is amazing. Where are they? And what genders?"

"I have two boys at the moment. I am so ashamed to tell you that the older one is aged eleven, and the younger one is almost turning eight. They are both at school now."

"My word, how time flies! It's okay, don't be too hard on yourself. You are lucky that we are still alive; anything could have happened in this long period of time. So what are their names?"

"The first one is called Tembani, and the second one is Sipho."

"Oh, those are very beautiful names. I hope I will meet my grandchildren soon."

"Definitely, Mum. Very soon."

"So, how far gone are you with this one?"

"Almost eight and half months."

"Nearly there, then. I can imagine the pressure on you taking the children to and from school. So, how are you managing?"

"It has really been challenging juggling the school runs and household chores on my own."

"Oh, is Pilani not helping you with the chores?"

Sindi just looked down on the floor in sadness. Her mother knew instantly things had gone wrong, but allowed her daughter time to gather the courage to tell her what happened.

"It's a long story, Mum. We are not together anymore."

"I am really sorry to hear that. I hope you are okay."

"Mum, the answer is no; I am not okay, but I am managing."

"I am really sorry that things didn't work out between the two of you. If you don't mind me asking, what exactly happened? You appeared such a great match."

"I guess looks are deceiving. Mum, I didn't know marriage was this hard. The last few years have been very challenging for me and the kids. Pilani changed overnight and became this monster I couldn't recognise. I should have seen the red flags at the beginning of our relationship, but

I was too focused on perfecting my marriage and pleasing him. From the moment we got married, he controlled everything I did. I did not have the means to contact you. That is not an excuse, but I didn't want to come back home to our poverty. I could not risk losing what I had. He threatened to leave me if I even visited you. All he wanted was for me to stay at home and prepare all his food for him."

Sindi's mum did not want to hurt her daughter's feelings by telling her that this was what she had feared might happen. "So, how are you managing financially?"

"I am on full benefits."

"There is no problem with that. As long as you're able to feed the children, that is okay."

"Thanks for understanding and not judging me. Mum, I came to ask you for a huge favour. I would like you to come and live with me for a short time whilst I prepare for the delivery of my unborn baby. I am really struggling at the moment."

"I can imagine! I would love to help you, but I will need to ask your father for his permission first. I hope he will understand your difficult circumstances and allow me to stay with you for the time you need me. Do you have a phone now?"

"Yes, Mum. I will give you my new number."

"Okay, I will ring you when I confirm what your father says."

"Okay, thanks. I need to get going now; I have to pick up the boys from school. It was really nice to see you again after such a long time, and sorry again for being a prodigal daughter. I will not allow such a thing to happen again. I have learnt my lesson now."

"No problem. Home will always be home, and you are welcome to come back anytime," Sindi's mother said. "On your next visit, please bring my grandchildren with you," she continued.

"Okay, Mum. I'm going to be late for the school run."

Sindi quickly scribbled something on a piece of paper. "Here, take this. It's my address and mobile number. I'll call you and tell you what time it is best for you to come. Even this weekend, if you are free when they are off school, how does that sound?" Sindi was starting to sound a bit stressed and moved towards the door.

"Okay, Sindi. Go, go, go! I'll catch up with you on your mobile," her mum said as she waved at Sindi while standing in the doorway.

Sindi left her mother's house and rushed to the school to pick up her children.

Sindi's mother was so pleased to be back in contact with her daughter and was looking forward to having a chance to spend quality time with her grandchildren she had not yet met. She was very understanding and did not judge Sindi for her absence. She clearly understood her explanation and was prepared to support her in this time of need. As a woman and wife, she empathised with her daughters' struggles.

She did not waste time getting in touch with Sindi the following day. She was delighted to give her daughter the good news that Sindi's father had agreed she could support Sindi for a short time whilst she prepared for the birth of her third child. Sindi was very pleased.

Sindi prepared the spare room for her mum. She did what she always did best: decorated it to make it look special using low-cost materials. When her mum eventually arrived at the agreed time, it was a surprise for the children to see their grandmother for the first time.

On the day her mother arrived, Sindi took her mother with her to her children's school. She needed to show her the route to the school and introduce her to their teachers for when she takes over during her maternity break.

The first child they picked after school was Tembani, and later, they collected Sipho.

"Hello there, young man, what is your name?" Sindi's mum asked.

"Tembani," he answered shyly, hiding behind his mum.

"And what is your name?" she asked, turning towards Sipho.

"Sipho, and who are you?" Sipho seemed more confident and asked curiously.

"Call me 'Gogo' or 'Ugogo,' which means grandma. Will you remember that?" she asked.

"Yes, that's easy. 'Gogo.' I will not forget that."

Turning to his mum, pulling her dress slightly and hiding his face from his grandmother, Sipho asked, "Mum, who is Gogo?"

"Okay, let's wait until we get home, and I will explain things to you."

When they got home, Sindi asked her sons to remove their uniforms and have their lunch.

"Sit down, both of you, and let me explain something. Right, you see this lady sitting next to me, who you're calling Gogo? She is my mother and will be staying with us for a short while. She will be helping me to take you both to and from school. Please be good to her, okay?"

"Yes, Mum," Tembani and Sipho echoed.

For the first time, the family shared a meal with their grandmother, and it was an exciting moment for them.

It became a usual routine for the family. The children were seemingly happy to spend quality time sitting with their grandmother, who enjoyed telling them fairytales. They looked forward to hearing more from her, especially at bedtime.

"Gogo, how come you tell us stories from your head, but Mum reads stories from books?" Sipho asked.

"I've got plenty of stories in my head, that's why," she answered.

"I like your stories, Gogo," Sipho said.

"Thank you, Grandson," she said.

When the children were at school, Sindi and her mother spent time cooking and baking like they used to when Sindi was living at home. The children always enjoyed having freshly made bread and cookies their mother and grandmother made. Sindi's mum had brought with her even more cooking recipes for Sindi to add to her already long list.

One day, whilst they were chatting away in the kitchen, Sindi's mum told her of a dream she had the previous night.

"Sindi, last night I had a very strange dream. I dreamt that Tembani had planted a big seed outside your garden. It had grown into a big plant, and it covered the whole house. Your house could barely be seen. I really don't know what this could mean."

"It could mean he will do something great," Sindi suggested. "But that's just my imagination. I'm really rubbish at interpreting dreams."

One day, as Sindi and her mum were relaxing and watching TV, her mum noticed that she was twisting and turning and making growling sounds of pain. She knew instantly that she was experiencing labour pains. She quickly gathered everything Sindi had prepared to take with her to the hospital and called an ambulance.

Fortunately, the delivery was quick and smooth. Sindi gave birth to the healthy, bouncy baby girl she had long waited for. Since there were no complications, Sindi was discharged the next day. The saddest thing was the absence of her husband. Sindi named her daughter Thandiwe as she had always planned, meaning 'The loved one.'

As Sindi walked through the front door with her new bundle of joy, Tembani and Sipho practically jumped on her, full of excitement. Sindi's mum beamed with joy to have the pleasure of seeing her third grandchild and how happy the other two were to finally have a sister.

Over the next few weeks, the family settled into a new routine, adjusting to a baby in the house. Sindi couldn't have asked for a better person to be with her at this challenging time. Whilst everything appeared to go seemingly smoothly for Sindi with the help of her mother, one day, her mother noticed that she looked spaced out, as if in deep thought, and she was very concerned about her daughter.

"Are you alright, Sindi?" she asked.

"Yeah...but no. There's so much going on in my head, Mum. I keep telling myself I am holding this beautiful baby, but her father is not in the picture. I don't know where he is or what he is up to. Since that fateful day when he left the house, he has not been in contact with me, made any effort to see his children or even posted a birthday card for them. I keep daydreaming of how great things were between us, and I just don't know what I could have done differently to save this marriage. I feel lost and empty inside. I keep asking myself, 'What happened?' and 'Where did everything go wrong?' I'm hurting, Mum, but I have to put on a brave face for my children's sake."

The sadness in her voice when she spoke touched her mother deeply. She knew she had to encourage her daughter to be strong.

"Sindi, look at me. I can feel your pain right inside my heart. I understand you're hurting, but right now, you have a lot on your plate. Stop blaming yourself. You are not responsible for Pilani's actions. What you did was very brave to put your safety and that of your children before marriage. Not many people can do that, so you need to be proud of yourself.

"In this crucial time in your life, I would ask you to try and shift your focus on what is in front of you right now, and that is the baby you're holding in your arms and the two beautiful boys you have. They love you, and you love them. You will make them sad if they see their mother sad. Please, focus on their welfare, and one day they will appreciate that their mother protected them from harm," her mother said.

"I guess it's hard to just brush things aside without going through the whole emotional process. Yes, Mum, I will work hard to overcome my doubts and fears. Thank you for supporting me in this difficult time," Sindi said.

"Come here."

Sindi's mum gives her daughter a warm, beautiful hug.

"Hey, Sindi, on a brighter note, I don't know if you've noticed that Tembani loves tidying up. I have also observed him paying a lot of attention to that plant outside. He always goes outside to water it. When he is doing this, he just seems so happy and very focused, and it's actually intriguing. It reminds me of that dream I had of him," Sindi's mother said.

"When our relationship was good, his father used to spend quality time playing football with him in the garden. I guess he is keeping himself busy and distracted by shifting his attention to the garden. So, which plant are you talking about, Mum?"

"That one just below your window outside," she said, pointing at the plant. "It is good that he can use a distraction technique at his age. Keep encouraging him to do that; it is certainly good for his mental well-being."

"I guess so. What I have also noticed is that he is super tidy, like his father. My Pilani was very immaculate and wanted things in their right places at all times," Sindi said.

"So he definitely takes after his father because that's exactly how he is coming across," Sindi's mum said.

They both laugh.

Sindi and her mother later enjoyed chatting together about life issues. In one of their conversations, Sindi informed her mother that with the birth of Thandiwe, she was really struggling to make ends meet. She didn't mention to her mother that even her presence at her house had added an additional expense, but she knew she needed her and did not want to risk being alone at this crucial time in her life.

As her struggles as a single mother intensified, and with no other means to cope, Sindi decided to apply for child maintenance from Pilani. However, her actions caused what she didn't anticipate. When Pilani discovered that the money he was earning was nearly halved due to child maintenance for the three children, he became very frustrated, and this exacerbated his drinking problem. As a consequence, there were increased reports from his colleagues and students that he was turning up to work smelling of alcohol and slurring his words, hence not fully concentrating on his work.

Therefore, Pilani was dismissed from his teaching job and was unable to hold any other meaningful job after that. The dismissal did not just affect him; it also had a severe impact on Sindi and the upkeep of her children. With no money coming from her maintenance claim, she struggled even more to support the children and her mum. Sindi was left with no choice but to politely ask her mum to leave.

She asked her to come whenever she wished and to continue to spend quality time with her grandchildren but not to stay. Her mum understood her daughter's situation and left. She visited Sindi on a regular basis and also invited her and the children to spend quality time with her during weekends.

When the maintenance money stopped, in a desperate effort to get answers, Sindi decided to go to her ex-husband's workplace to find out why he had stopped the payments. It was then that she discovered Pilani had been dismissed from the school for turning up to work smelling of alcohol.

She desperately needed the money to buy Tembani a new school uniform for secondary school, and this proved to be impossible. She went to the high street to get him a white shirt and grey trousers. Tembani already had a blue jumper that was part of his school uniform from his primary school, but it had holes in it. His shoes were torn and tattered, but Sindi had made an effort to apply super glue to mend them.

Tembani had got used to spending time playing with soil in their garden, admiring his plant that he was looking after to pass the time. He did not have the pleasure of owning a game console like other children his age, and spending time in the garden had become his new hobby.

CHAPTER ELEVEN

Tembani's childhood emotions are triggered

The first day at secondary school was not the greatest for Tembani or any child to ever experience as their first day at school. During his first assembly, he stood out for all the wrong reasons. He faced a lot of bullying from his first day for wearing torn shoes and carrying a torn rucksack. He watched other students pointing at his shoes and laughing. This made him feel sad and not want to be there.

Sindi was struggling immensely to afford to buy him essential school stuff that most children his age had, even though she always tried her hardest to give her three children a 'normal' life, regardless of their father's absence.

The behaviour of other students caused Tembani to distance himself from them from day one, and he was unable to make friends with them. He felt embarrassed and judged for what was not in his control.

When he got home, he could not wait to share the sad news with his mum about what had happened and how the other students had made him feel.

"Hey, Temba, how was your first day?" Sindi asked.

"Really horrible, Mum. Other students kept pointing at my shoes and laughing."

"Oh, I'm so sorry you had to experience this on your first day at secondary school. As your mum, I feel hurt that I could not afford to buy a new uniform for you."

"It's not your fault, Mum. You're trying your best."

"Where is Sipho?"

"Staying for afternoon activity; I will go and pick him up later. Anything to eat? I'm very hungry."

"I'll make you an egg sandwich and beans."

"Thank you, Mum. I'll go and change my uniform."

"Okay, quick, quick. I'll make you your favourite hot chocolate drink."

Okay, Mum, I'll be down in a sec."

After Tembani had his lunch, he went outside to check on his plant. This became a usual routine for him every day after school.

One day, in one of his classes, Tembani noticed a plant pot located by the window sills. His eyes instantly lit up. For the first time, he was seen smiling, and on this day, at the end of class, he asked his teacher if he could water the plant.

"Excuse me, Sir. Am I allowed to water that plant by the window sill?"

"Of course you can, and by the way, what is your name? I haven't grasped all your names yet."

"My name is Tembani, Sir."

"Beautiful name: Tembani. Do you remember my name?"

"Yes, Sir. You're Mr Aloha."

"Good man. Okay, let me give you my empty water bottle to use. There is a tap just outside the class. You like plants, do you?"

"Kind of. At home, I look after a plant in our garden."

"Okay, young man. When you finish, just throw the bottle in the plastic recycle bin outside."

"Okay, Sir. Thank you very much."

At least on this day, he had good news for his mother, and she was happy that he was adjusting to his new school routine. From that day, Tembani adapted to being at school by attending to plants in all his classrooms.

Later that day, as Tembani sat outside his home, looking at his plant, he noticed that it had blossomed and looked green and beautiful. A thought occurred to him. *I actually like plants.* With this thought, an unusual energy filled his entire mind and body. An 'I CAN DO THIS' attitude started to build within him. *If I can do this to this one plant, I can do the same thing with all the plants and flowers in all my classrooms,* he thought, and that's how he started to adopt this routine for himself at the end of his classes. He used it as a distraction measure to cope with his inner emotions about some unanswered questions he was struggling to deal with on his own, as he did not know how.

As the weeks and months past, Mr Aloha observed Tembani sticking to the same routine. He checked on the plant in his classroom, and when the soil was dry in the pot, he topped it up with water to keep the plant hydrated.

As much as he struggled in most subjects, Tembani seemed to be comfortable and happy in woodwork class. It was the only subject he looked forward to attending because his teacher always praised him and validated his efforts. He enjoyed it when his teacher displayed the beautiful pieces that he created. This made him feel proud.

One day, he asked his teacher for a spare piece of wood, and his teacher asked him what he wanted to do with it.

"Sir, it's my mum's birthday soon, and I can't afford to buy her a birthday card. I would like to make for her something nice and special."

"What do you have in mind?"

"I would like to carve a heart shape and write the words 'I LOVE YOU MUM'."

"That is so thoughtful of you at this young age. Your mum will be very happy and proud of you."

Tembani looked down to the floor. "Thank you, Sir."

Tembani secretly made this beautiful piece of art and decorated it well. He presented it to his mum on her birthday.

Sindi was filled with joy and was so pleased to see how talented her son was. Since the time Mr Hardy had reported that Tembani was not doing so well academically, he did not seem to have regained the required standard compared to other children of his school grade. However, she never made the mistake of comparing him to his father. She wanted her son to be himself and not to put pressure on him to become someone else.

When Tembani reached the age of fifteen and was in year 10, he had still not discussed his father's absence with his mother. What stood out about him, even at this age, was a lack of self-confidence and self-esteem; he struggled to express himself with teachers and other students at school. He found it hard to make friends as he lacked social skills and was seen mostly in his own company in the playground during break times. Even at this stage in his education, no one at his school had bothered to find out the reasons behind his behaviour, including his teachers.

Tembani was growing up seemingly baffled, feeling as though an essential figure was missing in his life; in particular, he felt he lacked a father figure. It affected how he behaved, and he struggled to come to terms with discussing his emotions with his mother about his father's absence. He kept his emotions bottled up all the time and was unsure of the best time to address his true feelings with anyone, including his mother.

He loved his mother dearly and was very protective of her. He was unsure if discussing his father with her would be a good idea. He couldn't imagine what her response might be if he expressed his true feelings.

Tembani had grown up witnessing his mother work tirelessly to put food on the table for him and his brother, juggling household chores and taking care of his baby sister, Thandiwe, who needed a lot of her attention. His brother Sipho was, at this stage, too young to process things, and Tembani had thought it unsuitable to involve him in discussing his feelings.

One day, whilst on a school break, sitting alone on a school bench as he usually did, Tembani overheard a conversation from his classmates

that would change his inner emotions completely. His classmates, Tato, Ajeel and Stephen, were gathering near him, speaking loudly and excitedly about activities they had done with their fathers over the weekend.

"Hey! Tato, what did you get up to at the weekend?" Ajeel asked.

"My dad and I went out paintballing, and after that, we played a game on PlayStation, and I beat my dad at it. He tried his hardest, but he couldn't keep up with my speed," Tato replied with great enthusiasm.

"Wow, that's so incredible! So your dad plays on your game console with you? Man, that's so cool! Mine does not even understand how to use it," Ajeel replied.

Stephen quickly jumped into the conversation and said, "Well, my father and I usually walk our dogs at the park and play football with other people we always meet there. At times, we just jog together for exercise; he's really competitive. Last weekend, he was too busy helping Mum with house decorations, so we didn't go anywhere, but I wasn't really bothered because I was busy anyway, studying for our science test."

"Maybe we should arrange a sleepover at mine one of these weekends?" Tato suggested. "What do you think, guys?"

"Hey, that sounds cool, I'd love that," Ajeel said.

"I'll ask my parents if it's okay for you both to come over to my house and join me and my father for our weekend activities," Tato said.

"Cool, I'll ask my parents too for their permission. Fingers crossed they will let me come. I can just imagine it, man! That'll be so amazing for all of us to go out together," Ajeel said with excitement.

The bell suddenly rang to indicate the end of break.

"Come on, guys, our break is over," Tato said. "Let's get back to class before we get ourselves into trouble. You know how strict our science teacher is."

"They all are, mate," Stephen said.

The three boys laughed as they hurried to their science class.

Tembani also stood up to go to the science class, but his thoughts from this point on were all muddled up. The conversation he had just overheard between his classmates had really affected him. He was left feeling triggered, and he could not wait for school to finish so he could speak to his mum about his thoughts and feelings that, up to now, he had been keeping bottled up.

After class, and as soon as he finished checking up on the plants in his classroom, Tembani struggled to hold back his tears whilst going home. It was at this point that he experienced for the first time a flash in his memory of his father's voice shouting at his mum, and when he cried, he was yelled at to stop crying.

However, on this day, he felt defeated. His heart was pounding, and he started to run home. His school was at least half a mile from his house. He cried, running all the way. As soon as he got home, he stood briefly by the doorstep and made an effort to wipe off all the tears. The last thing he wanted to do was to cause his mother to be upset or worry about him. In his eyes, she did not deserve any more problems to focus on other than looking after him and his siblings.

When Tembani eventually entered their house, he had not realised his face was stained from the tears; he looked as though he had been caught by the rain outside.

"Good afternoon, Mum." Tembani greeted his mother with a very deep but low tone of voice, just like his father's.

He had reached the stage where his voice had broken, and he sounded identical to his father. This scared Sindi so much. Their likeness to each other was unbelievable. His height had sprung up, too, and at the age of sixteen, he had reached almost five foot eleven and was towering over his mother.

As he swiftly tried to go past her, Sindi was quick to notice, causing her to become very suspicious.

This is not his usual behaviour, she thought to herself.

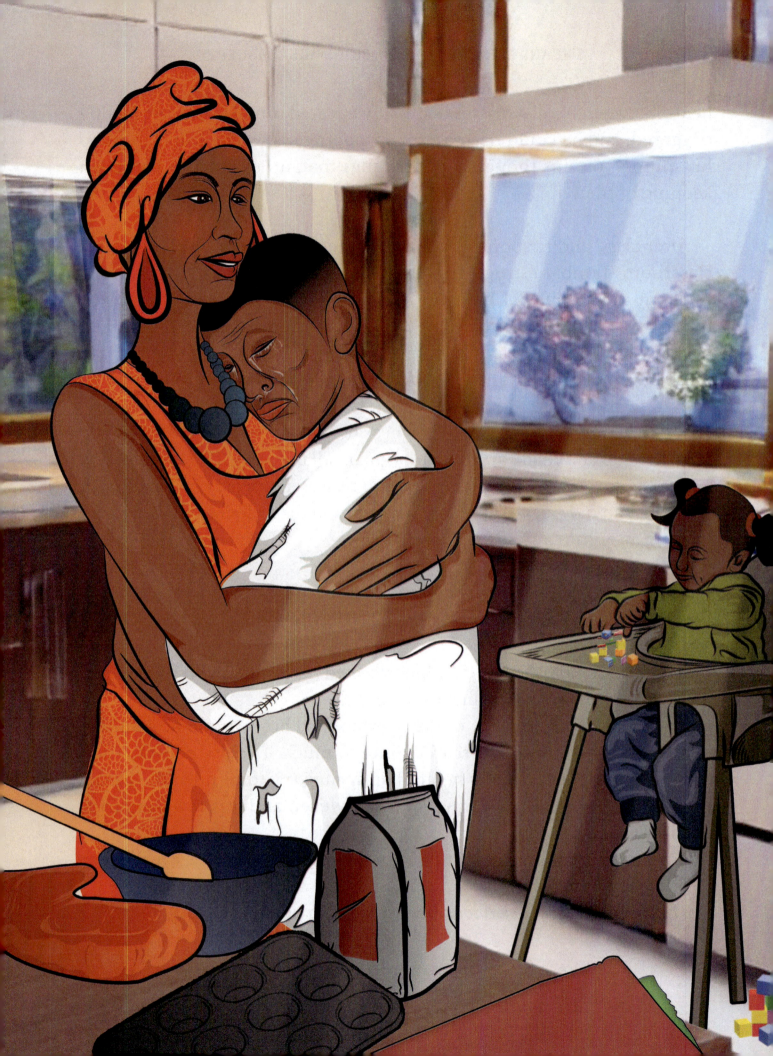

She turned around suddenly to face his direction as she had been in the midst of preparing a meal. As soon as she saw his face, she spotted immediately that he looked sad. Sindi instantly knew that something was amiss, and this sent a frenzy of emotions through her. She was very protective of her children, especially Tembani, as he was the oldest.

"Goodness me! Tembani! Come here, my son. Tell me, please, what's the matter? Did someone hurt you? Did you get into trouble at school? Please! Talk to me. What happened?" Sindi asked one question after another, without taking a breath. She was really worried about her son.

"Mum, please stop asking me so many questions!" he replied, and tears started to roll down his cheeks again.

"I am worried about you. You look drenched! Tell me, please! what happened?" Sindi was hysterical.

Tembani could not answer his mum for that moment. He started to sob even louder as his torn rucksack just slipped off his shoulders when he surrendered the tension of his body, giving up on trying to appear strong.

"Come on, Son. You can talk to me," she said as she helped him to put his bag down. "Take your time. Try to breathe in and out, okay?"

Sindi made every effort to comfort her son as Tembani's chest was visibly going up and down heavily.

"When you're ready, please tell me what happened," Sindi said.

She asked Tembani to sit down, and she sat right next to him and held his hands, which made him feel safe and comfortable.

Tembani remained mute for some time, breathing in and out as his mother had suggested, gathering his emotions together. Sindi was inwardly in a panic state, more than she was letting on, as she had never witnessed her son in such a state. She didn't know what to do at this point. She had to compose her emotions for the sake of her son in order to get answers from him.

"Whenever you're ready, Son, tell me what's going on." Sindi spoke in a calmer tone, but she had started to breathe fast herself as she was not getting any answers from her son.

Tembani gradually composed himself and gathered the courage to ask his mother a question any single mother would dread to be asked.

"Mum, where is my father?" Tembani asked.

Sindi immediately froze. She spontaneously paused and swallowed a large gulp of air, briefly struggling to answer the question whilst tripping her words in her thoughts. She immediately had a flashback of Pilani's voice saying to her, *'Remember, these are boys. One day, they will ask you where their father is.'* Now, that day had actually come. She had to think of how best she would answer her son's question without hurting his feelings.

After a brief moment, she replied. "Tembani, I asked your father to leave when things became very tough between us. It was a complicated matter. You're sixteen years of age now, and I believe I can explain things to you. Your father had developed a drinking problem; in actual fact, I would say alcohol addiction. Our relationship was tested intensely when the drinking caused him to become abusive both verbally and physically. I wanted him to go and get the help he needed, and at the time, it was the only option I had."

"Do you know where he is? Is he okay?"

"Tembani, I don't know where your father is, and it is sad that I don't know if he is okay or not. But I do hope he is."

"Why did you not ask him to get the help he needed whilst he stayed at home?"

"Tembani, it was very difficult. The saddest thing is that he did not think he had a drinking problem, and therefore, it was difficult to convince him to get help. As I said to you, my son, things were not good at the time. There was no communication left between us, let alone love for each other. All our communication had soured, and each day turned into bouts of anger towards one another. The worst thing was he had become physically abusive and would shout at you and Sipho for expressing your feelings when you cried. I could not watch both of you getting hurt anymore, and asking him to leave was my desperate measure to protect us."

"I see, and I am very sorry, Mum, that you had to go through all of this to protect yourself and us."

"First and foremost, I want you to know that your father was such an amazing person when we first met. He was a loving husband and father. Things gradually deteriorated between us when he developed a drinking problem. He disclosed to me a difficult upbringing with his father. He told me his father had too many expectations of him, and he did not want to let go of the old ways of looking at things.

"As a child, he felt all his efforts were thwarted. Orders were barked at him, and he was not given a chance to voice his opinions. The communication was parent to child, and a child had no say. This childhood trauma caused your father to form a relationship with drink, and this destroyed the goodness in him. I couldn't recognise the man he had become. I am very sorry that things turned out this way. It was one thing leading to another. He used aggression to prevent me from asking him about his drinking problem or whereabouts.

"His behaviour caused me to become a different woman. I was afraid it would affect my motherhood and parenting because I was always very upset and frustrated for not being heard. I used to scream at him in desperation, telling him to stop drinking and explaining what his drinking problem was doing to us. He would see my behaviour as an attack on him, and in return, he would physically assault me to keep quiet. The worst thing was that I was pregnant at the time, so I could not take chances with my then-unborn baby, your sister, Thandiwe.

"So, just to go back to your question, these are my reasons why I asked your father to leave, and I am sorry that I chose safety over love. Alcohol addiction took all that away; it took control of your father and took away the best in him. To continue loving him was as though I was in love with the wrong man. I am sorry that you have grown up without a father in your life because of your parents' choices."

"It's okay, Mum. I am sixteen years old and can understand where you are coming from. I guess as a young man, I just need answers and to know my identity. I am also worried about my father."

"Can you tell me what caused you to ask about your father today? You seemed tearful when you came home. Did something happen at school today that triggered your emotions?"

"I asked about my father because I overheard other boys at school talking about things that they do with their fathers. It made me feel sad, and I started to think, 'Where is my own father?'"

"I see."

"But thank you, Mum, for telling me all of this. Can I ask you something else?"

"Go ahead, Temba."

"Did Dad know you loved him?"

This question cut so deep into Sindi's heart because she knew the answer to her son's question, but she did not want to break down in his presence.

"I would like to believe that he knew I loved him very much, but unfortunately, he was in love with something else, and that was his alcohol."

"So, if he knew you loved him, why was he hurting you? Is it possible to hurt the people who love you?" Tembani asks innocently.

"Your father, who I know and met, loved me, but the addiction to alcohol took all that away. It hurts me up to now to believe alcohol destroyed my family. I can tell you to your face now that your father was such a loving husband and father before the addiction took control of him."

"Mum, I will never drink alcohol because I don't want to hurt anyone I love," Tembani said.

"Oh, that's so nice to hear." Sindi just smiled.

Of course, Tembani is still too young to commit to such a big statement, she thought to herself.

"But do you think Dad knew he had a drinking problem?" Tembani asked.

"I don't think so, my son, because he never accepted he had a drinking problem. Each time I tried to address the problem, he would become very aggressive and defensive, snapping at me for even raising my concerns. He would threaten me not to dare ask him about his drinking, and it was a scary moment to be around him," Sindi explained.

Tembani listened carefully.

"Your father had also started to come home in the middle of the night or not come back home at all from a night out. If he returned, he did not want me to ask him about his whereabouts. He would just go straight to the bedroom and sleep on the bed with his shoes on. I would have to tiptoe gently and remove his shoes for fear of being yelled at or even beaten up if I accidentally woke him up."

"That was some hard time you went through, Mum. I think you were very brave even to ask him to leave because he could have hurt you for asking him," Tembani said.

This image seemed to put him in a trance, and Sindi had to prompt him to continue.

"Temba, are you okay?" she asked.

"Now things are starting to make sense. Mostly when I am at school, I have been experiencing these weird flashbacks of exactly what you are describing, and I have been dismissing them, believing that I was just day-dreaming. I also easily lose my focus, and when the teacher is teaching, all I experience in my head are these loud noises. Even the school siren makes me jump. Sometimes, in my head, I hear Dad's voice shouting, and I also hear the sounds of things being thrown around the house. The feeling is just horrible and scary; it leaves me feeling so traumatised," Tembani said.

"It is important that you are able to talk about your feelings because bottling things in is not good for your mental well-being. Your father was prevented from voicing his feelings and thoughts, and look at what happened to him."

"Do married people hurt each other?"

"I'm afraid the answer is yes; sometimes, they do hurt each other."

"Did you ever call the police on him for hurting you?" Tembani asked a series of questions and was very worried.

"I never called the police on your father because I loved him very much and wanted to protect him."

"Protect him for hurting you?"

"Unfortunately, that's what love does. I couldn't imagine him going to jail and leaving us."

"But he is not here now."

"Remember, your father was a teacher then, and I did not want him to have a criminal record and lose his job. I did not work, and I did not want us to struggle. He would have blamed me for losing his job. I was really scared of the unknown; I was young and naïve, I guess. Besides, I was also very hopeful that he would change his behaviour."

"But, Mum, you're managing to look after us even now when you don't go to work. I know we're poor, but we're safe and happy, aren't we?" Tembani offers his mum a hug.

"You're right, my son," she said.

"Where did you get the courage to chase Dad away? I want to be as brave as you when I am older."

Sindi laughed briefly. "Let's get this fact right. I did not chase your father away. I asked him to leave and get the help he needed. Trust me, Son, it took me a very long time to gain the courage to stand up against the abuse. It was difficult because I had no one to confide in. I allowed myself to be isolated from everyone I knew, and I felt groomed to believe it was shameful to voice myself and share my problems with others, including my own family. My safety was compromised because your father put food on the table. At the time, I felt powerless and forced to do all he asked me to do, even if it was against my will," she ventilated to her son.

"That is so brave, Mum; I'm so proud of you."

"What happened between your father and I is sad because I believe there was true love between us. I want you to understand that he was battling a serious childhood trauma that caused him to have an alcohol addiction. This is a cruel illness that can change a person's life completely, their personality and behaviour. When the addiction kicks in, the people affected lose their sense of reasoning, causing them to end up unintentionally making wrong choices that hurt the very people they love and who love them. Your father used alcohol as a coping mechanism but lost control of it."

"I guess grandfather's behaviour was the reason Dad grew up to be the man he was? Am I right, Mum?" Tembani said.

"I guess if he had been given the opportunity to express his thoughts and feelings as a child, he would have dealt with things in a different way. It is good that we are having this kind of discussion now, because I don't want you to grow up thinking that your father was a bad person. But, his upbringing was a bit harsh for him," Sindi explained.

"All your father wanted was to follow his passion and become a gamer. He told me he enjoyed the challenge of winning games but only got the opportunity to do this when he visited his friends' homes because his father would never allow him to do this at their home or even consider buying him a game console. According to his father, playing video games was destructive and a waste of time. He never considered his choice as a prestigious profession to reflect on his own family's educational reputation. All of his uncles and aunts were highly educated people, mostly professors and lawyers, and had achieved doctorate levels. He thought your father choosing to become a gamer was definitely 'taboo' in his family, and he wanted him to acquire that same 'high status,' as he regarded it," Sindi explained.

"What is the meaning of 'taboo,' Mum?" Tembani asked.

"It means something that is not accepted by a certain custom or culture. In the worst case scenario, something that brings shame to the family," Sindi explained.

"I see," Tembani said.

"Unfortunately, at the time your father was growing up, he was not able to address these issues with his father, and this childhood trauma intensified. Later, this caused him to use alcohol to overcome these unaddressed childhood issues. Your father explained to me once that as a child, he felt silenced, and he was brought up not to question anything his parents said."

"Even if the child did not agree?" Tembani asked.

"That's right. A child remained a child and would not question an adult. This was regarded as being disrespectful and was a punishable offence. In one of his drunken episodes, he told me that I reminded him of his father, who was 'too controlling' when I questioned him about his drinking habits. To him, drinking alcohol made him feel good and in control of his life."

"I thought when someone was drunk, they would not know what they're doing."

"That's correct, Tembani, but what he meant was that no one would tell him how much alcohol to drink. Plus, when he was drunk, he felt that he was in control over himself, but of course, he was oblivious to what the drinking caused to his behaviour."

"That must have been a horrible feeling for him."

"That's correct. This is why I felt that if he left home, he would find the right help he needed."

"So, was he a good mathematician then?"

"I guess so. Once in a while, he used to come home and tell me about the praise he got from his headteacher. But like I said to you, he never liked his job. It was not his passion to become a mathematician. This pressure from his father to do what he didn't like caused him to form an unhealthy relationship with alcohol. The more he drank, the more problems he faced at school. He started to miss his teaching classes. This became so bad that he would go to work smelling of alcohol.

"One day, the headmaster called him to his office and told him of the complaints he had received from his colleagues and students, saying that he was attending his lessons smelling of alcohol. But, instead of addressing this issue, he decided to make threats to quit his job."

Tembani's eyes were glittering, with tears filling the bottom of his eyelids.

Sindi hugged her son and wiped away the tears using her apron.

"Look at me, my son. All these are scars from the beating I got from him for telling him what his drinking problem was doing to us." She lifted her sleeves to reveal all the marks she had been hiding away from her children.

"I'm truly sorry for showing you all this. I tried my best to keep this away from all of you as I did not want you to witness this, but I couldn't take being hurt anymore. I just wanted him to go and find the right support away from all of us..." Sindi broke down as she explained this to Tembani.

"I am really sorry, Mum, for asking you about my father and bringing back that pain. You never deserved to go through any of that, and I am glad you put yourself and your children first." Tembani moved even closer to his mother and gave her a beautiful, warm hug. He wiped away her tears using his torn school uniform.

"I am sorry, too" Sindi said. "That I cannot do the things your father would have done with you if he was here. I will never replace your father in that respect, but I will do whatever it takes to support you, your brother and sister in the best way I can. I know that one day, when you're older, you will be able to reach out to him and have the chance to get to know him and ask the questions you need answers to."

"Mum, I appreciate all that you do for us. I just wanted to have the answers that were bothering me. I didn't know how to express how I felt in the right way. Thank you again, Mum, for being there for us. Can I ask you a rather silly question, considering everything we're discussing?" he asked with a cheeky smile.

"Go ahead." Sindi closed one eye with her hand, unsure of what question her son would ask her this time around.

"Do you ever miss Dad?"

"You want an honest answer?"

"Of course, Mum, otherwise I wouldn't have asked the question."

"Frankly speaking, yes! I do miss him sometimes, but in my own way. Remember, he is still your father," she replied and gave her son a thoughtful smile.

"Thank you, Mum, for explaining things to me. I appreciate you being honest with me, and I will definitely look at things in a different way now," Tembani said.

CHAPTER TWELVE
Tembani reveals a deep secret

Tembani had other issues he needed to offload to his mother.
"Right, tell me, apart from what upset you today, how was school overall? I never got the chance to ask you. Do you have any homework?" she asked as she tried to change the subject to a lighter topic.

"School was okay, Mum, and thanks again for asking," Tembani said and immediately looked down to the floor. Another tear rolled down his cheeks again.

This time, his mother immediately used the paper towel that was near her to wipe the tears off and gave him another hug. She was very concerned for her son.

"Let it all out, Son; it is okay to cry. Please, tell me. What is the matter?"

"Well, to be honest, there is something else bothering me."

"Talk to me."

"Is there something wrong with me?"

"What makes you say that?"

"In most of my classes, I just seem absent-minded, unable to answer questions asked by the teachers as well as other children, and they always laugh at me for this. Is there something wrong with me?" Tembani asked his mum.

Sindi suddenly remembered the conversation she had with Mr Hardy, his primary school teacher, who had noticed a change in Tembani's concentration in class years ago. *I thought he had overcome this when she asked Pilani to leave*, she thought to herself.

This was the first time Tembani had revealed he was having problems at school, and Sindi felt disheartened as she knew what had caused her son to struggle with his learning. She was torn as she did not want to bring up the fact that it was the violence he experienced as a child that impacted his education. To Sindi, revealing this as a cause of his learning difficulties would build resentment towards his father, and she did not want this to happen between father and son. Sindi did not want history repeating itself for her son. The chain of events had to be broken. This revelation had come as a surprise to her. Tembani had never asked for help with his homework since starting secondary school, making Sindi believe that he was coping well at school.

"I feel so stupid and embarrassed when I compare myself to other kids. This makes me not like school very much. I only look forward to going to water the flowers and plants. This just makes me smile. I love flowers, Mum, and I always look forward to doing this after class. That's the only time I've heard a teacher recognise my efforts and praise me. It makes me feel good and appreciated, like I am good at something." Tembani shrugged his shoulders. This was the string of hope he was holding onto.

"Good on you. So you like plants and flowers? That is amazing! Who knows? One day, maybe you will become a horticulturist!"

"What is a horticulturist, Mum?"

"Someone who looks after plants and flowers. In actual fact, your grandmother once dreamt of you growing a seed that covered the whole house!"

Sindi and her son giggled.

"But, Mum, you keep saying you never went to school, but you bake these amazing cakes and yummy bread. *AND* you make super tasty soups as if you follow a recipe. The dinner ladies at school don't even make food that tastes as good as yours."

"Oh, stop flattering me!" Sindy said, chuckling loudly. "I don't follow any recipes, Son. My mother taught me very well. You saw how good her cooking and baking were when she came to stay over. I will share the tips with you one of these days."

"Woah! That will be amazing, Mum! I would really love to be as good as you. I can impress someone one day," Tembani said with a cheeky smile.

"But how come you always encourage me to go to school and to work hard? Can't I stay home with you and bake cakes all day?"

"No chance, Tembani. You need to go to school because you've got the opportunity to do so. I want you to do better for yourself, and I know you can."

"Mum, what are we having for lunch today? Something smells amazing in here," he declared, rubbing his hands together in excitement and diverting his mum's attention away from his problem at school.

"Guess what? It's your favourite pumpkin soup and fresh bread I baked this morning," she said.

"Yum, thank you, Mum. You're the best!" he said whilst dancing.

Tembani really enjoyed his meal and later spent some time with his young brother and sister.

Sindi's mood was affected following the discussion about Pilani with her son. She felt confused about whether she had left it too long to address Tembani about his father. She had been waiting for the right time, but was always unsure.

When is the right time, in actual fact, the right time? was a conflicting thought lingering in her head.

CHAPTER THIRTEEN

Mr Aloha observes Tembani's unusual behaviour

The next day, Tembani went to school as usual. Despite all that Tembani was facing emotionally, his unusual secret passion for plants and flowers was growing inside him every day.

Up until this point, no one had paid much attention to his pattern of behaviour. It would be regarded as an unusual fascination because not many students of his age would pay as much attention to watering plants and flowers in their classrooms as he did. However, Tembani really enjoyed doing it and always had a smile on his face. It was one of the only moments you would see him at ease and at peace with himself. Witnessing these plants and flowers come back to life brought a sense of hope and fulfilment in his inner self. He just naturally adored their beauty and everything about them.

Despite being poor and his uniform torn and tattered, Tembani was still able to maintain a smart appearance as much as possible. Apart from watering plants and flowers, he loved tidying up desks; it was fair to call him a neat freak. Unfortunately, Tembani struggled to recognise all these positive things about himself. He felt pressured to focus mainly on things other people believed he *should* be good at and that others *were* good at. His behaviour after classes continued to baffle his fellow students and, most of all, his teachers. They all wondered why he loved to water plants with a smile on his face, despite not getting any reward for it. The rowdy students picked on him for doing what made him happy. They would also wait for him outside the classroom to pull faces and laugh at him.

When some teachers heard about this bullying behaviour, they made sure it was addressed and dealt with, as it was unacceptable. Those caught faced detention and were given warnings as a way of stopping the bullying behaviour against Tembani and others.

After a while, most teachers started to pay attention to Tembani's behaviour and his routine after school. Some teachers encouraged it, whilst others asked him to put more effort into his schoolwork. In their opinion, this was not part of his school curriculum, and they saw Tembani's passion as a clear waste of time.

One of the teachers who observed Tembani's behaviour and was amazed was Mr Aloha. One day, he asked Tembani to speak to him after school.

"I notice that every time the school bell rings, you continue to remain behind to water all the plants and flowers on the windowsills. Why do you do this?" he asked.

"Sir, I just enjoy looking after plants, and that is all I am good at." Tembani suddenly looked down at the floor as if ashamed of his behaviour.

"Hey, please don't look down, Tembani. You should be proud of what you do, alright?"

"I understand, Sir, thank you."

"Hmm, will it come as a surprise to you that you are not only good at taking care of the plants? A little birdy told me that your woodwork teacher is very proud of you. He tells other teachers how gifted you are in his subject, so it seems to me, Son, you're gifted with artistic hands, too. What are your thoughts on that?" Mr Aloha asked, smiling.

"I am very pleased to hear that, and I am also pleased to know that you like what I do," Tembani exclaimed. Inwardly, he was surprised that Mr Aloha approved of what he was doing.

He smiled shyly and looked down at the floor again. He was also moved to hear that Mr Aloha had referred to him as 'Son.' For so long, he had longed for a male figure to call him 'Son.' This really made him feel like a man, and he was very excited. From this point, he was just grinning to himself.

"I can confirm to you now that you are very good at looking after the plants in all your classrooms, and you are a very neat and tidy young man. Well done! Look behind you. At one point, all those plants were dying until you started to take care of them. This is super impressive work, and I am very proud of you."

"Thank you, Sir,"

Mr Aloha thanked Tembani for coming to his class. Just before he left, he noticed how badly torn and tattered his uniform and shoes were, but he thought of a plan to help him.

When Tembani left Mr Aloha's class, emotionally, he felt like a different person. He was filled with energy, a feeling he had not experienced before. He set off to head straight home, a different skip with each step he took. As always, he only ever did this when he was in a happy mood, which was rare for him. On this day, Mr Aloha had made a significant impact on the way he felt about himself.

Unfortunately, this feeling would only be short-lived. As usual, the naughty students waited eagerly for him outside of the classroom to pick on him and make rude gestures at him.

"Tembani, look!" one of them shouted out and pulled a funny face at him.

On this particular day, Tembani put on a brave face and was not going to allow this bullying behaviour from his peers to affect how he was feeling at that moment. His thoughts were preoccupied with the nice comments Mr Aloha had given him, and he did not allow any negative thoughts to change that.

Tembani was keen to get home as fast as he could and share the good news he had received from Mr Aloha with his mother.

As soon as he got home, he just swung the door open and frantically said to his mum, "Mum, Mum! Mr Aloha said he was happy with what I do at school and proud of me. And guess what? He referred to me as 'Son.'"

"Aaaw, bless him. I wish to meet him one day. You always speak highly of him. He seems like a very lovely person," she said.

Tembani just smiled and was so talkative throughout the rest of the day. He got changed and ready to have his meal. Afterwards, he played with his siblings like he always did after school.

Sindi was pleased to see Tembani smiling and happy after a school day. She wondered whether the bullying he once reported to her was no longer a problem.

"Tembani, have those students who were taunting you stopped bullying you?"

"Mum, don't worry about it. I can handle it; I'm a big boy now. Look at my muscles!" he said, rolling up his shirt sleeve and flexing his bicep. "You will not always be there to protect me. Besides, the teachers have been supporting me, so yeah, they have stopped making jibes at me."

"I was just asking because I will not tolerate that behaviour from anyone. Bullying behaviour has no place in our society."

"Thank you, Mum, for always being there to support me."

CHAPTER FOURTEEN

Mr Aloha, the advocate

As Tembani's usual pattern of behaviour at school continued, Mr Aloha could not keep his thoughts to himself about him any longer. He felt it was about time for him to discuss what he had observed with other teachers and see what their thoughts were.

It was in the midst of a teacher's meeting in the staff room when Mr Aloha braved himself to catch his fellow colleagues' attention.

"Hey, guys, can I have your attention for a bit, please? Has any one of you noticed a certain behaviour from our student Tembani? I mean, those of you who teach him?" he asked.

The first teacher to speak, Mr Jones, responded with a dreadful laugh. "Oh my goodness!" he said. "You mean that student who always sits at the back of the class and never gets any answers right?"

The second teacher, Mrs Watsu, echoed almost the same thing. "In my class, I notice that he's very quiet. He just sits there and never says a word, and I never see him talk to other students, you know. I'm not sure if he's just normally rude or antisocial. You know these young students can be weird at times."

The third teacher, Mr Kwame, said, "All I have noticed is that after classes, he always cleans up after everybody; I guess that is all he is good at," he laughed. "I wonder if his parents know that this is all he comes to school to do?"

Mr Aloha's heart just sank hearing all his colleagues giving such negative feedback about Tembani and none of them focusing on his strengths.

He felt very disappointed by their perceptions. They all seemed to speak negatively about Tembani's behaviour.

One teacher called Mr Connor asked in a rather sarcastic style, "Mr Aloha, may I throw this question back to you? What have *you* observed Tembani doing that has caused you to bring his name to our attention?"

"Well, I guess the same thing as all of you have observed, but I look at his behaviour in a positive way, although I could be wrong. He remains behind after classes to attend to the plants. When he's doing that, he looks so focused, and his passion for plants and flowers is extraordinary. I find this behaviour more intriguing than his inability to participate as well as other students in my class," Mr Aloha said.

"So what is intriguing about his behaviour, if I may ask?" Mr Connor said. "Watering plants and flowers? Seriously, Mr Aloha? You've been a teacher for many years. I thought you'd know that this is not what we stand for as teachers. Our students come to school to learn, not to water plants and flowers.

"Please, teachers," he continued. "Correct me if I'm wrong, yeah? What Mr Aloha is suggesting to us is that we should all take notice of this student's passion for watering plants and flowers. More than encouraging him to concentrate on his studies?" Mr Connor strongly argued.

"Mr Connor, if *I* may correct you there, that is not what I am suggesting to any of you, but I am asking all of us to take notice of his behaviour. I think he deserves to be acknowledged and praised for what he is doing. He seems to take joy and pride in what he does, and it is our duty as his teachers to validate such efforts and make him feel valued and appreciated," Mr Aloha said.

"But isn't this the kind of thing he should be encouraged to do at home and definitely not at school, Mr Aloha?" another teacher said.

As this conversation turned into a heated debate amongst the teachers and seemed to go on forever, Tembani's woodwork teacher, Mr Bowdy, chipped in. "Come on, guys. In my class, Tembani is such an amazing student; if I'm being honest with you, he is actually one of the best. He makes such outstanding pieces. He is such a talented young man, and I agree with Mr Aloha that his behaviour should not go unnoticed. But I also totally agree that his school work should be encouraged just as much."

This compliment from Mr Bowdy made the other teachers feel embarrassed for only speaking negatively about Tembani's behaviour. Mr Aloha was not ready to give up, and he took this opportunity to ask other teachers what they were doing to help Tembani improve.

"Since we have all noticed that he is not achieving expected grades in most of the subjects, what efforts have we made to support him?" Mr Aloha asked his colleagues.

The maths teacher, in shame, quickly volunteered to offer Tembani extra lessons after school. One by one, other teachers also offered the same support for Tembani. Mr Aloha was very pleased that at least something positive was being done to support him rather than just criticise his behaviour.

Mr Aloha continued to address his colleagues. "On a different note, for all his time at this school, I have also observed that his uniform looks torn and tattered, and his shoes have holes in them. I don't know how we can support him to preserve his dignity and make him not feel humiliated by asking him for his uniform size. He may even ask why it took us this long to notice this and may not feel comfortable talking about it," he said.

"Don't we have spare uniforms in the lost and found property storage?" one teacher asked.

"Hmmm, I would rather we just get him a new pair of uniform and shoes. What do others think?"

"I guess it is never too late to help him," another teacher agreed.

After all the discussions about Tembani's behaviour and school uniform needs, all teachers agreed to make a small contribution towards this cause.

At this point, no one doubted that it was a good cause, but no one was confident enough to find out why Tembani's family could not afford to buy him a new school uniform or question a reason for his rare behaviour that they were debating.

After a long and exhausting discussion about Tembani, Mr Aloha thanked his fellow teachers for taking their time to discuss the student's issues, but he was not completely done with his colleagues. Without warning, Mr Aloha asked his colleagues what seemed to shock most of them.

He cleared his throat. "As you know, I am Tembani's form teacher, and I would like to support him in what he is doing. Is there any chance we can offer him a project to look after the school flowerbed and plants at the front of the school?"

"Huh?"

Confused sounds were heard from other teachers, and their facial expressions suggested Mr Aloha was not being constructive.

Mr Aloha was not ready to give up all efforts to convince his colleagues. He was more than determined to campaign for his colleagues' votes and continued. "Do we remember how the school front used to look some time back? The plants and flowers were all colourful, but now they look dry and gloomy. I believe if Tembani supports Mr Kona, our grounds maintenance staff, that will help. What do you think, guys? I suppose Mr Kona would be pleased to have a student he can guide in the maintenance of the school front."

Some teachers shook their heads in disbelief at what they were hearing.

"Mr Aloha, that is the role of the school: to employ more grounds maintenance staff rather than allow a student to do that. I find your suggestion ridiculous and, in my personal opinion, out of order. I would certainly not allow my child to do this. Hell, no!" one teacher exclaimed.

"This is what he seems to enjoy doing. Tembani is not being forced to do what he does not like. I will speak to him and hear his opinion on this offer. He will just be focusing mainly on the school front and not the whole school. I believe this will make him happy as he enjoys looking after plants and flowers. This could even form part of his work experience since he is nearing the end of his secondary education," Mr Aloha insisted.

"Shouldn't this idea come from him rather than you, Mr Aloha?" another teacher voiced their opinion.

"I agree with what you have just said. However, as a student, I don't think he knows that this might be an option that could be offered to him at this school," Mr Aloha said.

"Mr Aloha, may I just remind you that Mr Kona works here and Tembani is a student! How can we allow our student to take up such a challenging task like that without even the approval of his parents?" a teacher asked.

"I guess this is something we can discuss with Tembani and his parents if he's happy to do this," Mr Aloha said. "It is not just about the school front but offering Tembani the opportunity to do what he seems to love doing. Besides, he is almost at the end of his semester. Who knows how this experience might benefit him in the future?" Mr Aloha explained.

He made all efforts to convince his colleagues that Tembani was the best person to do this project, based on the natural care he gives to the plants and flowers in their classrooms.

"Can any of us argue that the plants in our classrooms were all dying, and thanks to Tembani, who started to take great care of them, they are now looking extremely beautiful? He definitely has a great passion for plants and flowers," Mr Aloha said, seemingly desperate to win his colleagues' support annoyingly to some of his colleagues.

"So, why can't we offer him a bigger project and see how well he manages his passion for plants and flowers?" he suggested.

One teacher, Miss Nanku, coughed rudely and murmured something from under her breath. "'Passion,' my foot." She then addressed Mr Aloha. "So, what you're saying, Mr Aloha, is that this student is 'special' because he waters plants in our classrooms, and now they look 'great'? Hello? I'm sorry to say that I certainly do not agree he is 'special' in any way, especially in that respect."

"Of course, Miss Nanku, you're entitled to your opinion, but I stand by my word. I certainly believe there is something special about

Tembani. He is very good with his hands. It's like whatever he touches turns to gold," Mr Aloha emphasised.

"Really? What exactly has he turned to gold?" she uttered. She was speechless, and she just rolled her eyes in response to Mr Aloha's praises of Tembani.

In a last desperate effort to convince his colleague to support him with his motion, Mr Aloha stood up from where he was sitting. The whole staff room went silent and looked in his direction to find out what on earth he was going to say this time. In their minds, there was absolutely nothing that he could say to convince them that Tembani was 'special' because of his passion for flowers.

Mr Aloha paused for a while and said, "Come on, guys. Let's help this student. Your support really matters. I cannot do this alone." He sounded very worried.

After careful thought, one teacher asked, "When will he get time to do this, Mr Aloha?"

"After school, the same way as other students have time to do their extra-curricular activities. He may enjoy attending to plants and flowers instead of playing on the field," Mr Aloha said. "I get it, guys. This is not something we have dealt with before, but there is always a first time," Mr Aloha said in excitement.

"Tell me, how many students of Tembani's age would spend their time watering plants and flowers after lessons instead of playing with their mates? He clearly takes joy in what he does, which indicates that he is dedicated to doing it," Mr Aloha said.

He continued. "May I also bring to your attention, if you've not already heard about this, the news of other students bullying him for his love of watering flowers? If this was something he did not care about, I'm sure he would have submitted to the bullying. As teachers, we need to protect him and show our support," Mr Aloha said. This time, his voice was shaking due to his desperation and the lack of support he was still getting from fellow teachers.

Some teachers were really getting frustrated listening to Mr Aloha's campaign for Tembani and had decided to leave the staff room as they did not wish to participate in this debate any longer. Mr Aloha was very disappointed by this reaction from his colleagues, but he clearly was undeterred from helping Tembani in what he believed was a good cause. He continued to speak highly to the teachers who had chosen to remain in the staff room. Inwardly, he feared that his hopes to help him were fading.

As if oblivious to what had just happened, Mr Aloha said, "If we agree to allow Tembani to do this project, I will ask him, with the headteacher's permission, if it is something he would approve a student to do at this school. I will also ask Tembani to seek permission from his parents if they will support him in doing this project."

Mr Bongani, the headteacher, who was present in the staff room for all this while and had preferred only to listen and not to interfere in this debate, decided it was now time to politely interrupt.

"Teachers, may I have your attention, please? I think you have all said what needs to be said. Would you allow me to speak now?" Mr Bongani turned to face Mr Aloha. "Mr Aloha, I hear what you are saying, and I will certainly support your motion. To the rest of the teachers, I can also understand where you are coming from, as we have never dealt with such a situation at this school before. However, having listened to all sides, the most important person here is Tembani. We will need to figure out how he will feel to be offered such a project. And secondly, it will be important that we seek his parent's approval if they support the cause. On this note, I would ask for your vote either in favour of this proposed idea or against it," Mr Bongani said calmly.

There was an immediate awkward silence from the room. Immediately, there was a lot of murmuring in the staff room.

Some teachers could still be overheard talking between themselves. "Has Mr Aloha lost his mind? This is a boy who is achieving extremely

low grades in all his academic subjects. He should not be encouraged to water plants and flowers but to concentrate on his academic studies."

On the other hand, some teachers argued if any help would make any difference. Most teachers had concluded that Tembani was not gifted in the area of academics and saw no bright future for him after he left school.

As this debate seemed to continue, Mr Bongani had to put a stop to it. He put pressure on the teachers to reach a final decision to vote, either in favour of or against the proposed idea by Mr Aloha. Eventually, one by one, the teachers hesitantly lifted their hands up to vote. Some supported the idea of giving this chance to Tembani, whilst others were against allowing him to take up this gardening project as it was a further clear distraction to his studies.

After the votes were finally counted, miraculously, there was just one additional vote in favour of allowing Tembani to take up this gardening project. So, in the end, it was finally agreed to give this young student the opportunity to do what he did best and enjoyed doing.

At school the following day, Tembani finished his last lesson in Mr Aloha's classroom. As usual, he set himself to complete his routine of watering flower pots. He was about to say goodbye to Mr Aloha, who had been patiently waiting for him to finish so that he could take the opportunity to speak to him about his proposed idea.

Mr Aloha said, "Tembani, I would like to start by thanking you for being consistently hardworking watering the plants after lessons. It is an amazing thing you do."

"Thank you, Sir," Tembani said, as always shyly.

Mr Aloha went on, "I have a proposed project for you, young man, but only if you are happy to do it."

Tembani's eyes opened wide, thinking to himself, *God, what project could Mr Aloha ask me to do when I am not good at anything?*

Mr Aloha then asked Tembani, "How would you feel if the school asked you to oversee the watering of the flowerbeds and plants at the front of the school? I mean, pruning the plants and flowers and watering them after school?"

Tembani was quiet for a moment, as if in utter shock, but eventually, he responded timidly and with a slight stutter. "Sir…I…I feel so honoured to be given this chance to do this project. I love looking after plants and flowers. At home, I do this, but our yard is very small. I'd be very happy to do the project, Sir. Thank you, Sir."

Mr Aloha smiled and said, "That's it then, Tembani. I will support you all the way once you get permission from your parents, okay? Once you get that, I will then arrange for you to get all the tools you need," Mr Aloha continued. He was not aware of Tembani's home situation: that he only lived with his mother and his siblings.

"Yes, Sir, and thank you so much for your support," replied Tembani.

As Tembani headed towards the door, Mr Aloha said, "Before you leave, I just want to let you know that some teachers have offered to help you catch up with your school work, and you will be given a new set of books so you can study at home. Is this okay with you? As teachers, we're also going to buy you a new uniform and a pair of shoes. What's your thought on that?"

"Thank you, Sir. I really appreciate that," Tembani replied. Inwardly, he felt a bit embarrassed that teachers had only noticed his torn uniform now, but at the same time, he was pleased with their offer.

Deep in his thoughts, Tembani was very pleased with the support he was getting from the teachers who were willing to encourage him with extra lessons and study books to read. Secretly, what excited him the most was the gardening project Mr Aloha had proposed because that is where his passion lay. Tembani could not wait to get permission from his mother to do this. On this day after school, Tembani felt very excited, and he celebrated by striding joyfully all the way home.

Mr Aloha watched Tembani striding away, and he, too, felt very happy and was smiling to witness his student in such a jovial mood. He felt like a proud father at that moment. Meanwhile, he arranged all the equipment that he would need to kick-start this project. He was hopeful that Tembani's parents would give him permission to do this project.

CHAPTER FIFTEEN
Tembani shares good news

Tembani could not wait to get home and share this amazing news with his mother. When he eventually got home, he just dropped his school bag to the floor and rushed to embrace his mother.

Sindi was amazed by this reaction from her son, and she said, "You are beaming with joy! Tell me, what happened today at school?"

"You will not believe this, Mum! Mr Aloha asked me to take up an after-school project to look after the plants and flowers at the front of the school!"

"Oh my goodness, that's exciting news! Your grandmother will be so pleased to hear this because she has always told me how much you like to water and look after your plant outside. She always said you look very happy when you do this. I am thrilled that your teacher has taken notice of your passion. This will be a great opportunity for you to do what you enjoy doing. Well done, my son. How do you feel about it?" Sindi asked.

"I am over the moon, Mum; I love plants and flowers. I really can't believe this is happening. I'm very pleased you are supporting me to do this," Tembani said with excitement.

"You know I would always love to support you. As long as *you are* happy, I certainly do give you permission to do this! But I have just one question to ask you. Will your teachers be happy with you doing this? And will this project not interfere with your learning?" she asked.

"Mum, please don't spoil it for me. Remember, I will be doing this after school, so it won't affect my studies in any way," Tembani responded.

Inwardly, Tembani knew his capabilities and realised that no matter how much time he spent on his academic work, he would not be able to achieve the grades expected of him.

Sindi was so delighted to see her son in such a happy mood for once after a school day. As always, she gave him a big warm hug.

"Make us all proud and make your teachers proud, especially Mr Aloha," Sindi said.

"I promise you, Mum, I won't disappoint him, and thank you again for allowing me to do this. I was pretty nervous you would not give me permission," Tembani said.

"My pleasure. Now, come on. Go to your room and take off your uniform. Don't forget to have a good shower, okay? You definitely need it after all that running," Sindi said, joking with her son.

Tembani made a gesture to smell his armpit, and he quickly went to the bathroom to have a shower. He was prepared to do anything that would not make his mum change her mind.

As soon as he finished showering, he sneaked out to their front yard to check his plant. He spent time practising gardening skills outside in his mother's yard, but since they did not have the flowers to plant, Tembani just made the empty flowerbed in front of his mother's house look very lovely and neat. He just watered the one plant. Sindi looked admirably at what her son was doing through the window. Tembani was unaware his mother was watching his every move. Sindi just smiled and was so impressed with what she saw. Tembani had made the yard look immaculate, as if there were actually flowers there. Sindi was so impressed with what her son had done in a short space of time, but she had kept this to herself.

For the first time, Tembani could not wait to go back to school the next day. He could not stop imagining how he would start this project. He was very happy but anxious, too.

"Tembani, you've worked so hard today. Tell you what? You deserve your favourite baked bread and soup, hey? Come on, please have some rest. Call your brother and come and sit down at the table. Eat whilst the food is still hot," Sindi said.

"Thanks, Ma. You're always the best," Tembani said.

Time seemed to be at a standstill for Tembani on this day. He just could not wait to go back to school and share the good news with Mr Aloha that his mother had given him permission to do the gardening project that he had proposed.

Tembani's excitement was so great that he even shared the news with his younger brother and sister, who had no clue what he was talking about. Nevertheless, they smiled when they saw their brother happy. Happiness was written all over his face. Tembani went to bed earlier than usual.

In the morning, he was up early. He was the one who woke up his mother, and it was usually the other way around. He was over the moon to start this project.

"Tembani, you look so excited. Slow down a bit! Remember the saying 'More haste and less speed'?" Sindi said.

"Okay, Ma! But I'm just so excited to get to school today," he said.

Inwardly, Sindi was proud to see her son look forward to going to school in such a happy mood.

CHAPTER SIXTEEN
Tembani begins his school project

That morning, Tembani left home to go to school earlier than usual. The first thing he wanted to do was to find Mr Aloha and tell him the good news that his mother had given him permission to start with the school project.

When he finally found him, Tembani greeted his teacher with so much enthusiasm.

"Good morning, Sir!" he said.

"Good morning, Tembani. You seem very bright this morning. I hope you have good news for me," Mr Aloha said.

"Yes, Sir! I spoke to my mum yesterday about the gardening project, and she gave me permission to do it. She was very happy for me. She thinks I will be great at the job," Tembani said, still smiling.

"Congratulations, young man. Come and see me after school to kick-start the project," Mr Aloha said.

"Thank you, Sir; I can't wait. I'm so nervous but excited at the same time," Tembani said.

"You will be fine. Don't worry too much," Mr Aloha reassured Tembani.

Mr Aloha had never seen Tembani in such a bubbly mood. Inwardly, he was very proud of him and had now witnessed the other side of Tembani that he never displayed when he was in class.

After school, Tembani maintained his daily routine of tidying up the classroom and watering the plants and flowers in the flower pots. He met Mr Aloha at the garden shed where all equipment was kept. Mr

Kona, the head of maintenance, was also present to meet Tembani for the first time.

"Tembani, meet Mr Kona, the head of maintenance. He will be guiding you to know your tools and how to handle them safely. Mr Kona, please meet Tembani. He is the student I spoke to you about. He is very passionate about plants and flowers, and I trust you will guide him along the way, teaching him about tools and everything else he needs to know about plant and flower upkeep. Most importantly, how to use and store the tools safely," Mr Aloha said.

"Hello, Tembani, nice to meet you. I have heard so much about you from Mr Aloha. Of course, I'll be very pleased to show you all you need to know. I hope you will enjoy your project. Please don't be afraid to ask any questions, okay?" Mr Kona said.

"Nice to meet you, Sir." Tembani stretched his hand out to greet Mr Kona.

"My pleasure. Thank you, Mr Aloha, I'll take over from here," Mr Kona said.

Mr Aloha walked back towards the school building.

"So, let's get started," Mr Kona said. "Mr Aloha told me all about you and how much you love plants and flowers. How did this passion come about?" he asked.

"I really don't know how to explain it. I just love them, and it is a natural feeling I have for them. Just looking after them, seeing them bloom and come to life, makes me very happy," Tembani said.

"I'm sure the plants and flowers will be happy to see you, too."

They both laughed light-heartedly.

"Lately, I have been very busy maintaining the football pitch, preparing for the school tournaments around the corner," Mr Kona explained.

"Okay, I see," Tembani responded.

"Right, Tembani, first things first. I will show you all the tools you will need and how to use them safely, okay?" Mr Kona said.

"Yes, Mr Kona," Tembani replied.

One by one, Mr Kona showed Tembani all the tools and how to store them safely when he finished using them.

"Always wash all the soil off the tools so that they don't get rusty. That is what happens if you leave the soil and mud on them," Mr Kona told Tembani.

Tembani listened attentively to everything he was being told.

"So, tell me, are your parents happy with you doing this?" Mr Kona asked.

"My mum has given me permission. She knows I love plants and flowers. She just asked me to be safe using the tools and not to get carried away and get home late," Tembani responded.

"Definitely. I will make sure you keep to a timetable and time. I will make sure you always finish on time, okay?" Mr Kona said.

"Thank you, Sir," Tembani said.

"I am very pleased to see a young student of your age developing a strong passion for plants and flowers. This is the first time in all the years I have been here. Good on you. Not many students your age will make time to do this. Instead, they prefer playing football or other sporting activities," Mr Kona said.

"Well, I am no good at any sports anyway," Tembani said and immediately looked at the floor as if ashamed.

"Listen to me, young man. What matters the most is that you are happy with what you are doing. Always remember that 'It is okay to be different,'" Mr Kona said as he patted Tembani on the back in encouragement.

"Right, let's get started. I will show you the area I want you to focus on, which is mainly at the front of the school. As you know, once in a while, we get some important people visiting the school, so it is very important to keep the school front looking nice," Mr Kona said.

He asked Tembani if he was sure of taking up this school project whilst he was still studying.

"Are you sure you really want to do this? It will not be very easy, let me tell you that," Mr Kona said.

"Yes, Mr Kona, I am sure. I am up for the challenge, and I believe you will guide me along the way, won't you?" Tembani said shyly.

"Of course, I will guide you; that's not a problem," Mr Kona said.

Mr Kona demonstrated how to use the tools in a safe manner and asked Tembani to do likewise.

"You are coming across like a natural to me with these flowers; well done. I'll leave you for now, but if you need me, you will find me near the football field where I am working today," Mr Kona said. "I know you're very excited to do this, but please give yourself time to rest, and you need to be finished by 4 o'clock so that you don't go home late, alright? I don't want your parents to be upset that you're leaving school late on your first day!" Mr Kona said.

"Okay, Mr Kona", Tembani said excitedly.

Tembani started off very well, pruning the roses. He dug up the edges of the flowerbeds and removed all the dead leaves from the ground. He finished the day by watering the flowerbed. Seeing what he had done in his first session, he felt pleased and proud. He cleaned all tools before he put them away in the garden shed as he was instructed by Mr Kona and finished for the day.

Tembani made sure he said goodbye to Mr Kona.

When Tembani had left, Mr Kona went to take a peek at what he had done on his first day, and he was very impressed with what he saw. In his heart, there was definitely something special about the way Tembani had just started with the project. Each day, he gave it his all to ensure the flowerbeds were neat and tidy. He would neatly put away the tools as Mr Kona directed him.

Weeks passed, and this routine carried on for some time.

CHAPTER SEVENTEEN

A transformation that will mark history

After a few months had passed, positive results started to show how hard Tembani had worked on the school front.

As the headteacher, Mr Bongani, entered the schoolyard one morning, he was astounded by what he saw. He noticed something quite unique, unusual and breathtaking. The school flowerbed had been transformed, and it looked absolutely gorgeous and stunning. All the flowers had blossomed, and gorgeous-looking butterflies were flying majestically above the flowers and the whole schoolyard. It was as though he had entered a new school. His heart was filled with joy, and he could not wipe the grin off his face.

Mr Bongani seemed transfixed at the entrance of the school, beaming with pride for what his student had achieved, defying all odds. He moved his head from side to side, enjoying the new school view. It was breathtaking. He was not the only one taken aback by this new transformation; his fellow teachers and students were, too. They all shared the same reaction to what they saw.

For the first time, large, beautiful and colourful butterflies of all kinds were seen flying proudly all over the schoolyard. Bumble bees and honey bees were also hovering over some clusters of plants. The students were seen running happily around the schoolyard, chasing the butterflies, trying to catch them. Everyone who entered the school just smiled. The building was filled with a beautiful scent of flowers. For the first time at this school, everyone praised Tembani's name. He was talked about in a positive way by everyone who entered the schoolyard and witnessed this amazing sight. He felt very proud that all his efforts had paid off.

Mr Bongani could not help but call for an emergency meeting with all the teachers to discuss this amazing transformation of the school entrance. As the teachers started to gather in the staff meeting room, Mr Aloha, who was also present, could overhear his colleagues echoing the same thing: 'How the school flowerbed had been transformed into something beautiful.'

When all the teachers had gathered in the staff room, Mr Bongani asked them to sit down to explain why he had invited them for this emergency meeting, even though, to some, it seemed obvious.

"Good morning to you all!" Mr Bongani greeted the teachers with much enthusiasm.

"Good morning, Sir," all teachers echoed.

"I called this meeting to discuss what I witnessed today as I entered the school front," he said enthusiastically.

The teachers nodded their heads in agreement with what Mr Bongani was saying.

"Wow, ladies and gentlemen! I am actually feeling quite emotional right now. I think you will all agree with me that this young man, Tembani, has surprised us all. The work he has produced at the front of the school is first class. I can now agree with the saying, 'Give a child a tool, and they will learn to use it.'

"Tembani has far exceeded my expectations. The flowers look colourful and spectacular, and all plants look amazingly green and beautiful. I have never seen so many beautiful butterflies at this school," Mr Bongani said.

All the teachers started to murmur in agreement with Mr Bongani.

"Since we have witnessed this student's efforts and agree that he has produced such an amazing work, we cannot just leave it here. It is our duty to acknowledge his efforts. This could be significant in how he feels about himself and what he likes doing. I would like to nominate you, Mr Aloha, to inform Tembani of how much we appreciate the effort he has put into the appearance of the school. I can honestly say I have not seen such a wonderful display of so many beautiful flowers since I have been head here. I would urge him to continue doing this when he leaves school. Who knows where this could take him? I feel rejuvenated within myself, and for once, I feel proud of entering my school. The significance of butterflies is also a very good sign. They symbolise new beginnings and growth," Mr Bongani said.

All the teachers in the staff room applauded.

Mr Aloha was delighted to be nominated to pass this appreciation on to Tembani. After the teachers' meeting, Mr Aloha could not help but feel very proud of Tembani. He could not wait to share this amazing news with him.

Mr Aloha waited until the end of his lesson to tell his class what the meeting he attended was about. "I have an announcement to make," he began.

All the students started to pay attention.

"I guess you all witnessed something spectacular this morning when you entered the schoolyard. Is that right?" Mr Aloha said.

The students nodded their heads.

"Can anyone tell me what you noticed?" he asked.

"I saw a lot of butterflies and bees," one student answered.

"Yes, yes, yes," an echo came from other students in class.

"Okay, okay, let's keep the noise down. There are other classes going on next door," Mr Aloha said. "I just want to share some great news with all of you. Mr Bongani met with all of us this morning and asked me, in particular, to thank you, Tembani, for the outstanding work you've done to transform the front of our schoolyard," he explained.

"May we clap our hands for Tembani, please?" Mr Aloha said.

There were scattered sounds of claps heard coming from different parts of the class. Not every student was amused by this announcement. As some students clapped, others chose not to for personal reasons. Other students decided to be even more dramatic and chuckled annoyingly, facing Tembani. This reaction affected Mr Aloha deeply and caused him to become very upset. He paused for a bit, and after he had gathered his composure, he asked the students who had been chuckling to explain themselves.

One of the students responded and said, "Really? Is this something to announce to us and to be proud of? Watering school flowers? Come on, Sir," he said, laughing.

The other students who felt the same way also joined in the laughter, which truly infuriated Mr Aloha so much. However, he was a very experienced teacher, and instead of focusing on these disruptive students, he refocused his attention on Tembani, who was clearly affected by the reaction of his classmates.

"Tembani, I would like to congratulate you on your hard work transforming our schoolyard. You have shown great determination and resilience. Good lad, keep up the good work," Mr Aloha said.

"Thank you very much, Sir," he responded, but immediately started to cry.

Seeing how the reaction from fellow students had affected him, Mr Aloha immediately asked the disrespectful students to leave the classroom, not as a punishment, but to reflect on their behaviours.

As the rude students remained outside of the class, Mr Aloha continued to praise Tembani.

"As I was saying, the flowers at the school front were looking dry and brittle, but thanks to you, young man, you have brought them back to life and transformed our school. We are proud of you, well done," Mr Aloha emphasised.

Another round of applause began, and this time, more students clapped than before.

Tembani felt encouraged and started to smile.

"How many of you love butterflies?" Mr Aloha asked in excitement.

"Me, me!" echoed the other students.

As Mr Aloha continued to shower Tembani with praise, some students still believed his achievement had no relevance to their learning. However, they did not dare show this to their teacher, fearing they would be asked to leave the classroom like their classmates for expressing their opinions.

Some students stood up and offered Tembani hugs of comfort; others just looked emotionlessly in his direction. Tembani was more affected by those students who didn't wish him well, and he soon started to feel unwanted and unappreciated.

Mr Aloha comforted him and told him it was okay to cry. Tembani started to experience a flashback of his childhood trauma when his father told him that 'Men don't cry.'

"Do men cry, Sir?" he asked Mr Aloha.

"Believe it or not, real men do cry. I cry sometimes. Does this surprise you? Crying does not make you less of a man; in fact, it makes you more of a man, do you understand? Come on, lift your head up high. What you have done is different and very special. It is something that has never been achieved at this school by anyone, let alone a student. Your classmates are young; they do not recognise where teachers are coming from in praising you for your extraordinary effort. How are you feeling? Come on, wipe away those tears," Mr Aloha supported Tembani.

After class, Mr Aloha called on the disruptive students and addressed them on the impact their behaviour can have on another student. Even after he spoke to them, they were still adamant that their teacher should not have praised Tembani for watering flowers and plants, as this was not why they came to school. Mr Aloha explained to them that their voices did matter, but he did not appreciate them making another student feel unappreciated and not valued. They apologised, and Mr Aloha allowed them back in class after they had reflected on their behaviour.

After school, Tembani still managed to stay behind to tidy up as usual, but his self-esteem and confidence felt exceptionally low. On this day, he noticed that there was more litter in class than usual. Tembani came to the conclusion that other students who were not happy for him had deliberately littered the classroom again to sabotage all his good work and make him feel small. He managed to pick up all the litter and finished with his gardening project. After he completed all his chores, Tembani ran home crying.

When he got home, his mother asked him frantically, "What's up, Tembani? Why are you crying?"

Tembani was in floods of tears, and at that point, he was unable even to answer his mother.

"Did someone hit you? Tell me, please, what happened?" She was desperate for an answer.

"Mum, Mr Aloha announced to the class today that the school front was looking beautiful because of the gardening project I am doing. But other students started to laugh at me, saying that was not something to be proud of," Tembani explained, his voice choking from the tears.

"I am really sorry to hear this, but that is far from the truth, my son," she said. She placed her hands on his shoulders and said, "Tembani, look at me. Your teacher praised you because he saw the amazing work you have done. You love your plants and flowers. Don't be sad, but continue to do what you love. Try to focus on the people who see you for who you are, okay?" Sindi said.

"Can I make you a nice hot drink? And my special bread is here today. How about that?" Sindi comforted her son.

"Thank you, Mum. You're always so nice. I love you so much," Tembani said with a smile and wiping off the tears.

Sindi made him a nice hot drink and served it with a warm, freshly baked slice of bread and butter, which was his favourite. After the first sip of his favourite drink, he smiled at his mother.

"Thanks for always supporting me when I'm down and not judging me for being too emotional," Tembani said.

Later, Tembani gathered courage and told his mum everything that had happened in class with his classmates. He began to explain that they felt Mr Aloha was being trivial for praising him for this sort of thing. On top of laughing at him, they had also littered the classroom in protest at the praise he got from Mr Aloha.

His mother could not help but share Tembani's pain. She hugged him again and said, "Son, look, you're growing up to become a man and re-member, men cry too, but they become stronger every time challenges are thrown at them," Sindi said. "You have made me proud; you have made your teacher proud. Most importantly, you are doing what you en-joy doing best. That is what matters," Sindi continued to comfort her son.

She helped him wipe off the tears from his cheeks and said, "Son, do not be disheartened. Carry on doing what you love. You will get the re-ward you deserve one day for all your hard work and efforts. Continue to follow your dreams," Sindi said.

Tembani felt so much better after getting this warm response from his mother.

After this conversation, he felt an extraordinary strength, determina-tion and confidence building within him. He could not wait to go back to school to continue with his new project.

CHAPTER EIGHTEEN

A transformation like no other

The next day, when Tembani went to school, he felt like a changed young man. He carried on with his school project as before and did not allow the bullies to affect his progress.

The difference Tembani had made to the schoolyard was so immaculate and outstanding that Mr Bongani decided to approach other teachers to discuss how they could incorporate his achievement into the parents' evening, where other students' recognition in different subject areas would also be announced. Most teachers acknowledged that recognising what Tembani had achieved would inspire other non-academically gifted students to do likewise and follow in their dreams. A large assembly for teachers and students was arranged.

The big day arrived. All the students and guests were seated in their designated places in the school hall. Mr Bongani began by welcoming everyone. He announced how important this day was to the school. After he read out the agenda of the meeting, one by one, he called each student to come up to the stage to award them with their certificate of achievement in their respective areas. When it was Tembani's turn, he started by asking a question.

"Before I call this student to the podium, I would like to ask you something. What changes have you noticed at the front of the school?"

"The butterflies...beautiful flowers...bumble bees..." Different responses from teachers and students of what they had observed echoed around the room.

"Well done, and I agree with all of you. The next student I will call up on stage in a few minutes has not just achieved all of what you have testified just now, but he has also brought great awareness to this school of what following one's dreams means. In all my years of teaching, I have not come across such an inspiring student. He has taught me the meaning of resilience, focus and consistency.

"The area in which he has excelled is a subject by no means taught at this school. This young man is self-taught. He has shown me as the head of school that if you give a child any tool, they will make something out of it, and he is clear evidence of this. When a teacher approached me and told me about this student and his love for flowers, I will be honest with you: I was not convinced. Now I can stand in front of you and say how wrong I was."

A round of applause came from the audience.

"I would like to call Tembani to come up to the stage," Mr Bongani declared.

Tembani walked up to the podium.

"The reason I have called Tembani to the podium is that this young man has done something that has never been accomplished at this school before. He volunteered to attend to the plants and flowers at the front of the school and has exceeded our expectations."

Some boos were heard coming from some students who were not happy with the showers of praise Tembani was getting.

"Thank you, thank you, settle down, please." Mr Bongani did not want this negative response to disrupt his speech.

"I will continue if you will allow me to." He cleared his throat before speaking again. "I have been a headteacher at this school for many years, and I have never seen this school look this remarkable. I understand why some of you are not happy with this praise because we don't have a subject in gardening. This is the reason I have asked for your attention to acknowledge the efforts this student has made without any guidance from any one of us. This is a rare example, and I hope Tembani will teach other students what he has taught himself. I would be happy to add a gardening project to our extra-curricular activities."

Applause and whistling filled the whole hall.

"Thank you, thank you. On behalf of the school, Tembani, please kindly receive this certificate of achievement. I would like to say don't give up on your dream even after you leave this school. Well done, young man."

Tembani took the certificate from Mr Bogani and turned to start walking away.

"Before you sit down, I have another certificate to award you for being the best student in woodwork. You're very talented with the skills of your hands. Keep it up."

Tembani received his second certificate.

"Thank you, Sir," he said and left the stage.

There were a few teachers who preferred to remain silent and were also sceptical of why Tembani's achievements deserved so much praise. They believed only those students who were high achievers academically deserved this accolade, not merely watering plants and flowers. To them, this was not part of the school curriculum and had no place to be recognised as 'special' or associated with any part of school achievement. They believed this gesture would deter high-achieving students from working hard in their academic work.

However, Mr Bongani had directly announced to the whole school that what Tembani had done was extraordinary, and placed a strong emphasis on the importance of recognising all-round talent.

Tembani's achievement remained a debatable issue at the school for a very long time.

After two years had passed, it was now nearing the end of Tembani's secondary education and time to leave school. He felt so sad to be leaving and stopping doing what he enjoyed doing best. What he didn't know was that Mr Bongani and Mr Aloha had a surprise for him up their sleeves. To thank him for all his hard work maintaining the schoolyard and making it look beautiful during his time at the school, they had secretly bought him pots and seeds for plants and flowers of all kinds to take home as a special gift.

Mr Bongani called him to his office to break the news to him. He encouraged him not to stop loving his gardening project but to continue to plant more flowers at home in his mother's yard. It was as though Tembani had won the lottery.

After school, he went home at full speed, bursting with excitement. He quickly decided to borrow his mother's old wheelbarrow to go back to school and pick up the flower pots and plants he had been given by Mr Bongani and Mr Aloha. Tembani was about to do what no other student had done after leaving school.

CHAPTER NINETEEN
Tembani, the unexpected entrepreneur

It wasn't long until Tembani had started to transfer all the gardening skills he had learnt at school to his mother's yard. His passion for plants and flowers gradually started to show when he planted beautiful flowers at the front of their home. Their yard was not as big as the school's, but Tembani still managed to transform his mother's empty flowerbed into one that was adored by everyone who passed by his house. Tembani's mother and his siblings were amazed at how Tembani had quickly renovated their yard within a short time.

In the limited space of their yard, Tembani gradually created a beautiful small greenhouse in their back garden using scrap wood he got from various carpentry workshops he visited. His woodwork skills were now coming into effect. He frequently visited the nearby furniture-making workshops to request scrap wood to make ornaments and keep himself busy. He was always lucky to be given a few scraps of wood that he carved into unbelievably beautiful objects.

He started to sell some of them at the market, and to his amazement, people loved his work, and they sold fast. This was so encouraging for Tembani, who had very little hope of getting a job after completing school. He earned a few pounds to spend and helped his mother to buy some ingredients for her baking. It was at this point that his mother noticed how talented her son was. His passion for artwork grew by the day.

Nine months had passed since Tembani left school, and everyone who went by his house was astounded by the transformation of his mother's front yard.

One day, a neighbour who could not help but admire the flowers she saw outside the yard decided to speak to him as he was busy working in the flowerbed.

"Hello, Tembani!" the neighbour said.

"Hi, how are you?" Tembani responded in a deep voice.

"Is this all your work? Wow! Your flowers look spectacular! I have been walking past your house almost daily, and each time I pass here, I see big changes. What's your secret? Where did you learn to grow flowers? You are so good. Well done. This is pure evidence of a fantastic job."

"Thank you so much for the compliments."

"I definitely want mine to look like yours. Any chance you could help? Of course, it won't be for free; I'll pay for the services."

"I'll get back to you about that," Tembani responded with a big grin on his face.

"You're a seriously talented young man; keep it up."

"Cheers."

This was the first time anyone had asked to pay him to do a gardening service. Unknown to Tembani, this was only the beginning of a life-changing experience that was about to unfold for him.

Tembani shared the news with his mother, and she was pleased for him. She gave him the go-ahead to charge their neighbour a small fee to transform their yard. Besides, the family were so broke they could not afford to decline such an offer.

The work he completed for his neighbour impressed her so much that she suggested he start advertising his services using flyers. She offered to help him to do this. Tembani took her advice on board, and from that moment, he was hired almost on a daily basis. From being a young man who did not have a job, he suddenly became very busy doing people's gardens. He was so good at what he did that all the people he offered his services to recommended him to others. Tembani's life started to transform faster than he could have imagined, almost unrecognisably.

His mother's house began to look like one of those you would see in magazines, not like a typical house you would see on a council estate.

As the demand for his flowers and gardening services grew, Tembani decided to rent a place at the marketplace to grow more flowers. He made amazing flower pots and planted different types of flowers in them to sell. Buyers always came back for more. The demand grew, and he started to hire other people to help him meet the ever-growing demand for his gardening project.

The word regarding his immaculate work spread like wildfire in his town. Everyone wanted a piece to make their gardens and venues look great. He always delivered high-standard work. Money started to roll in gradually, and he treated his mother, brother Sipho and sister Thandiwe to their first shopping trip.

Sindi was so proud of her son's achievements. She shared the brilliant news with her mother and jokingly called her a 'witch.' She reminded her of the dream she had of Tembani growing a seed, and now the dream was coming to life. Sindi invited her family to visit her regularly since she was no longer short of food to share with them.

Tembani could not believe how his life was transforming right before his eyes. He remained humble and did not allow this to affect his work. His first purchase with his savings was material to build an even bigger greenhouse in the market shed. His flowers and objects were so attractive that all his produce and creations were sold out on a daily basis. His success became renowned in his town, and within a short time, he had saved enough money to put a deposit down on a penthouse to move into, with more land to grow his produce.

CHAPTER TWENTY
Tembani transforms from boy to man

Five years went by after Tembani left school. By now, it was clear how he had improved his family's life. His flower business expanded rapidly, and he started to be famous for growing the most beautiful plants and flowers in his town. He became the biggest supplier of flowers to shops, wedding venues, parties of all kinds, churches, private homes, shops, funeral parlours, online shopping, greenhouses, and schools for their special occasions. His company became the go-to for all functions.

Tembani became a leading employer in his town. He was loved by all the people who worked with him. He was kind and considerate and was determined to encourage his employees to become entrepreneurs and to follow their dreams as he had done.

One day, as Tembani reflected on how far he had come, he decided to honour his mother for being his rock since his father left their home. He waited until her next birthday to make the occasion memorable for her. Unbeknown to anyone, he had also been working secretly, crafting a special present he would reveal on the day.

This gift meant a lot to Tembani, and he could not have considered giving it to anyone besides his dearest mother. In preparation for her birthday party, he invited his grandmother and people he considered inspirational and influential to his success. He appreciated his humble beginnings, and to add to his list of guests, he invited his former teachers, Mr Aloha and Mr Bowdy in particular.

In order to make this day extra special and unforgettable for his mother, he hired a party planner. The house was well decorated beyond anyone's imagination. There were lovely melodies playing in the background to everyone's taste and a variety of food to choose from. All the people present were oblivious as what Tembani had up his sleeve.

When it was nearly time to unveil the secret gift to his mother, he reached into his pocket for a blindfold. "Before I put this blindfold on you, Mum," he said, "I have a little speech to make that I prepared earlier on, especially for you."

Everyone stopped what they were doing and listened.

"Mum, first of all, I would like to wish you a happy birthday, and if I had the power, I would grant you eternity. You're a special woman, and I am so proud to call you my mum. You are a strong woman, and your resilience to hardship is priceless. I wish everyone here could have had the pleasure to live with this woman and witness the great things she did and continues to do for her children. As a child growing up, I saw my mother single-handedly juggling parenthood and housekeeping, but she still managed to keep smiles on our faces every day. I never heard my mum complain, not one day. Even after I had a rough day at school, she always found the right words to cheer me up and was a great listener.

"You never judged me when I came from school complaining of all sorts of things. You've sacrificed your own needs for me and my siblings. You truly are one of the most selfless humans I know, and I am incredibly lucky. The gift I am about to present to you is to honour you and all mothers like you who go out of your way to put your children's needs first under all circumstances. I LOVE YOU, MUM, and I hope that this day will be one of your best." Tembani held his hand in the air to show his crossed fingers. "I have said enough for now; please come with me to the balcony. Guests, please follow me."

Tembani placed the blindfold over his mother's eyes and guided her towards the balcony.

"Tembani, you know how nervous I get when you do this to me. I'm not very good at handling pressure, let alone surprises. Please don't do this to me. Look at my chest; can you see it going up and down? You will kill me on my birthday. Look! You can literally hear my heartbeat. Please make it quick before I collapse on you."

"Hey, hey, Mother, trust me on this. Don't faint on me, though!"

The guests laughed, and Sindi sighed deeply.

On the balcony lay a large object that was covered with a beautiful cloth.

"My body is shaking," Sindi said.

"You'll be fine, Mum."

As soon as they all got to the balcony, Tembani put his index finger to his lips to signal all the guests not to make a sound.

After making this gesture, he then gently removed the cloth that covered the mysterious object.

All the guests could do was open their eyes wide in amazement at what stood in front of them. They were the first to witness this incredible, beautifully crafted wooden sculpture that stood in front of them. It was a statue of his mother holding a bunch of flowers. They all held their mouths to stop themselves from making any sound so as not to give anything away. Tembani carefully removed the blindfold from his mother's eyes. She was gobsmacked seeing an exquisite sculpture of herself standing right in front of her.

"Oh my word," she uttered. She just hugged her son so tightly.

"It's okay, Mum. There was no better way I could have expressed my gratitude to you. You're an amazing woman any child would be proud to call 'Mother.'"

"I'm speechless. Never in my wildest dreams did I ever expect that something like this could happen to someone like me. This is so beautiful. I am so proud of you, Son." Sindi turned to face her mother. "Mum, look

at what your grandson has done for me. Your dream, Mum, your dream has come true. I really can't believe this is happening to me."

"Well done, Tembani, for honouring my daughter in this way," his grandmother said.

Sindi remained rooted in one spot, holding her hands to her face, still in utter shock. Tears of joy started to run down her cheeks. Sindi could not control her emotions. The statue was outstandingly beautiful and shiny. Everyone present was moved and surprised by Tembani's talent.

Sindi continued to hug her son, sobbing for a very long time, and Tembani used his jacket to wipe off his mother's tears. This moved his guests greatly, and some of them shed a tear or two.

"Mum, do you remember when you used to use your apron full of flour to wipe my tears?" he asked, laughing. "Those were my tears of pain, and now I am wiping off your tears, but I believe these are tears of joy," Tembani said, smiling adoringly at his mum.

"Yes, Son, they're certainly tears of joy. I cannot believe you kept this secret away from me!" Sindi said as she hit Tembani lightly on the arm.

Mr Bowdy was similarly moved by this sculpture, which was absolutely beyond his expectations and also brought tears to his eyes. On the other hand, Mr Aloha was seen just beaming with pride and joy to witness what his former student had achieved since leaving school and following his dreams.

During the party, Tembani managed to catch up with both his teachers.

"Tembani, I am so proud of you," Mr Bowdy said. "That sculpture is to die for. Even with my years of experience as a woodwork teacher, I would not have produced such a beautiful piece."

"Thank you, Mr Bowdy, but don't take credit away from yourself because I learnt all the skills from you."

"You are too kind, but this is another level. Have you ever considered coming back to the school and telling your story to our current students? I'm sure they will benefit a lot from listening to you."

"I support that, Mr Bowdy," Mr Aloha said. "Your story, Tembani, will give hope to all those children who have been through tough times like yourself. They will also understand that it takes a lot of dedication and commitment to achieve what you have attained since leaving school," Mr Aloha echoed the decision.

This occasion and conversation made Tembani determined to go back to his former school to tell his story. He hoped to inspire other students with similar upbringings and, most importantly, the learning difficulties he developed after witnessing the domestic violence between his parents. He wanted to share his amazing life story with other students and the challenges he had to overcome to get to where he was. Tembani felt it was important for him to return and deliver a speech to thank his school for giving him this opportunity to become who he wanted to be. He wanted to thank especially Mr Aloha and all those teachers who took a leap of faith in him, spotted his rare talent, and above all, believed in him.

He planned carefully for this special occasion. He reached out to his former headteacher for permission to do this. When Mr Bongani received his request, he was more than pleased to have him visit the school for this undoubtedly inspiring story. He also extended his invitation to all students and their parents, of course, to all those who were willing to attend. Tembani wanted this to be a big occasion and mainly to raise awareness at the school to avoid making similar mistakes that could have hindered his success.

CHAPTER TWENTY-ONE
Tembani tells his story

When the day finally arrived, Tembani was very nervous about the thought of going back to his former school. He did not have a clue about what to expect from this day, but he was optimistic. He had been planning for it for some time. His aim was to bring awareness to parents and teachers by highlighting the difficulties he experienced as a student and what could be improved in the future to prevent similar occurrences.

When Tembani finally arrived at the school, Mr Bongani was already waiting to meet him.

"Hello, Tembani! You have not changed much. You look well," Mr Bongani said as he greeted him.

"Mr Bongani, thank you for accepting my request to come back to the school to tell my story. Yeah, really good to see you again, and I'll tell you what, you haven't changed a bit either," Tembani said.

They both shared a good laugh.

"Well, in this field, we are kept so busy with work and probably don't realise how fast time moves," Mr Bongani replied with a smile. "Come on in," Mr Bongani said, ushering Tembani and his team into his office.

After they sat down, they discussed the structure of the day. When everything had been covered, Mr Bongani took Tembani and his colleagues to the school hall, where he was going to address the school and the invitees.

The hall was beautifully decorated. All arrangements were set to suit this unique occasion. The first thing Tembani had noticed when he entered the school grounds was the absence of the butterflies, but he kept this to himself for that moment. The flowers at the front of the school had also dried up, and the beauty that was once there was no more. This view had saddened him, but he was prepared to bring this vision back to life. First things first, though, Tembani needed to prepare for the day and all that he had planned for this day.

As the assembly hall started to fill up, Tembani was ushered to sit at the front of the podium. When the ceremony began, Mr Bongani introduced Tembani to the school.

"Good afternoon to you, ladies and gentlemen. Firstly, I would like to thank you all for accepting my invitation to come here today. We have a very special guest amongst us today. His name is Tembani, and he has a mission to tell you all about his experience at this school and why he has decided to come back to share his story.

"Tembani, I welcome you back to the school. Please, come forward and introduce yourself to everyone," Mr Bongani said.

The audience began a long round of applause.

"Thank you for giving me such a lovely welcome, and a good afternoon to you all," Tembani began his speech.

"Good afternoon, Sir!" an echo came from the students, and they overshadowed the teachers and parents.

"Just call me Tembani, okay? 'Sir' is for the older guys sitting over there, okay? Do you agree?" Tembani joked, pointing in the direction of the teachers.

The audience laughed.

"I would like to start off by thanking Mr Bongani for accepting my request to come back to the school and meet you all. My name is Tembani, as Mr Bongani mentioned. I was a student here a few years ago, and I have come back here to share my story with you all."

An absolute silence fell over the hall.

"I am the firstborn of three children, and I was raised by a single mother for most of my life. She is sat over there, somewhere," he said, pointing somewhere in the audience. "I invited her to share this moment with me. I feel honoured that my mother, Sindi is her name, is present here today. I will confess that she was always very busy looking after my young brother and sister and never got the chance to attend any of my school parents' events. Never mind, that time is past," Tembani said.

"Life was not easy for her raising me and my two siblings. She separated from my father when we were very young. You can imagine how difficult it was juggling household chores, putting food on the table and making sure we attended school on time. It was really tough, bless her. She relied mainly on state benefits.

"Believe it or not, I wore a torn and tattered uniform on my first day of secondary school and for most of my time at this school. On a day when most children are proud to be part of the grown-up elite, for me, it brought, in fact, a feeling of shame. I wore a new uniform after teachers made a contribution to get me one, and thank you again to all the teachers who supported me. Some of you are still here, but some have left.

"Unfortunately, coming to school in a torn uniform came with a price. Not all students understood what I was going through. I was laughed at and experienced a lot of bullying for things I could not control. The students were too young to understand what I was going through at home. I isolated myself because I felt different from others. My self-esteem was compromised. I found it difficult to talk to people and left school without making any friends."

The audience continued to sit in silence.

"That being said, not everything was all bad, and I would like to thank Mr Aloha, who is sitting amongst those teachers," Tembani said, pointing in the direction of Mr Aloha, "for paying attention to my individual needs. I have to be honest with you all. Because of all these challenges I had to face, I hated school very much. What kept me coming back to school was my love for plants and flowers. To other students, this was uncommon and odd. To me, this was my happiest moment. Attending to flowers was like therapy. I smiled every time I saw the flowers blossom, and watching the butterflies flying above the school brought so much joy to my heart.

"Not all teachers approved of my passion. Looking back now, I can understand why my behaviour was considered unusual. No children of my age were doing this. Most of them were attending extra-curricular activities like football, basketball, you name it. But watering flowers? Come on! It was like, 'What on earth is this dude doing?'"

The audience laughed.

"In my heart, I always wondered, 'Do these children know how I feel?' I felt so joyful and at peace. The colours, scent and shapes of the flowers just caused me to be happy and smile. When I was offered the opportunity to look after the school front, my word! I felt a sense of belonging. Internally, it felt like, 'This is me.'

"Now, I can proudly say this determination and passion have paid off. I am now the proud owner of a large plant and flower company. I supply my produce to a lot of companies and retailers," Tembani said.

The audience clapped.

"My reason for addressing you is that I know that amongst you are students and parents who may be going through what my family and I have gone through. I was lucky to have this passion that has made me the man I am today, but not everyone has the same passion or experience. However, what I would say to any of you feeling hopeless if you are not as gifted academically as other students is 'Follow your dreams, whatever they are.'"

Tembani then turned to Mr Bongani, Mr Aloha and Mr Bowdy. "Thank you all for believing in me. You recognised my strengths and not my weaknesses; you focused on what I could achieve rather than what I could not achieve." A tear ran down his cheeks. "Without your support, all this would not have been possible," he said.

"I will share briefly how I felt growing up without a father. Life was hard, and I missed out on certain things that most boys do with their fathers. I never owned a game console. It was difficult to listen to boys of my age bragging about things they did with their fathers. The absence of my father in my life caused me to lack focus in my learning. Teachers have a big role to play in identifying kids like me in schools and supporting them in any way possible. Thank you all for listening.

"Finally, I am very happy to fund any child who is going through a tough time. I urge all those affected to speak to the headteacher, and I will take it from there. I would like to use this platform to encourage all parents to support their children, despite their talents, and not to compare them to their other children or siblings. Most importantly, observe any behaviours that may suggest they are being bullied at school, and explore reasons why your children hate going to school. That is important. There could be something more than meets the eye. I have said a lot, but before I sit down, does anyone have any questions?" Tembani asked.

One student stood up and asked, "With all of the flowers you grow, do you have any favourite flower or plant, Sir?"

Tembani cast him a funny look for calling him 'Sir' but quickly smiled.

"That's a very difficult question for me to answer because I love all my plants and flowers. They all represent different things: our love for each other, our mood, different celebrations, and sadly, some of them express how sad we feel," Tembani answered.

"Come on, Sir, there should be at least one that stands out. Tell me, tell me, Sir!" the student asked excitedly.

"Okay, okay, I'll confess to everyone now. The one flower I adore is called the lotus flower. Have you heard of it?"

"No, Sir. Tell us more, please," the boy said.

Echoes of agreement came from the hall.

"Okay. This flower is very special to me for a number of reasons. It stays in murky mud at night and rises from the mud in the mornings without any stains on its petals. Can you believe that? It's actually true. It happens every day. I find this very interesting and special. Also, I would urge anyone going through a tough time to relate to this flower." Tembani spoke with so much emotion.

"Why is that, Sir?" the student was keen to hear more.

"Right, like I said, this flower goes through a lot: murky waters and mud every night, but it still manages to rise up in the mornings, shining bright without any mud on it. I relate to this flower because a lot of different challenges are thrown at us in our lives, but we need to rise up to them and still be the best people we can, despite what is thrown at us," Tembani explained.

"Wow, that's so cool," was overheard from the students.

"Yes, it is truly amazing. This flower stands out for me, and I would like most of you to adapt its resilience," Tembani emphasised.

Another burst of applause was heard but was followed by a raise of a hand from one parent.

"Yes, Ma'am, what is your question?" Tembani asked.

"Tembani, it seems to me that you are encouraging our students to believe life is easy and that if they have a passion like yours, all would be simple for them. Don't you think this might deter students from trying hard at school, believing that if they adopt a passion for flowers, their lives will change?" the parent asked.

"Certainly not, Ma-am. Education is key in every child's life, but not every child is born academically gifted, and it is fair to give such children an option to choose what they are good at. The purpose of my speech is to encourage the minority of students who are not gifted academically not to lose hope but to follow their dreams where their passion lies. This could be singing, carpentry, cooking, literally just anything they love and have a great passion for. If they set their mind to it, then they will achieve their dreams. I just want those small groups of students who struggle in school to continue to have hope. I made it through my passion for flowers, but everyone is different," Tembani responded.

"Well explained, and thank you," the parent said.

"You are most welcome," Tembani said.

"I'll be very happy to speak to anyone after this assembly who would like to know more about my flower and plant projects or has any more questions for me," Tembani said as he prepared to sit back down in his seat.

A teacher was brave enough to stand up and acknowledge what Tembani was saying and addressed the audience about how he would look at the culture of learning in a different way going forward. One by one, the students and parents clapped for the teacher for this acknowledgement. One parent from the crowd also stood up and thanked Tembani for highlighting these difficult topics.

Mr Bongani closed the ceremony and promised all students and parents that, moving forward, the school will fund training for teachers to spot the students who present with differences and offer them the right care and support. He also encouraged students who experience bullying for being different to speak up both at school and at home in order to get the support they need.

At the end of this assembly, Tembani informed Mr Bongani that he had brought new plants and flowers with him. He vowed to provide a regular service for the school to maintain its flowers, free of charge. Mr Bongani was incredibly moved by this suggestion, and did not hesitate to take up the offer. He started to tear up when he began visualising the beauty of the butterflies that once flew around the school when Tembani was managing the school front. He could not wipe the grin off his face.

Lastly, Tembani donated a fund to the school to support those students from less privileged backgrounds to attain school material to enhance their studies. He also offered free training to all those students who wanted to follow in his career of flower and plant upkeep. He further offered to stock the lost and found storage with new uniforms and shoes of different sizes for those children from low-income families, as he did not want any other child to go through what he went through. Mr Bongani was very thankful to Tembani.

After the ceremony, the whole school enjoyed a lovely meal made by the catering company Tembani had hired for this special occasion. Tembani spent some time talking to the students about what changes they would like to see. Most of them were delighted to speak to him and vent their own struggles. Tembani advised them to speak up and address any issues to the head of the school for the right support.

CHAPTER TWENTY-TWO

Unfinished business

A couple of months later, Tembani arranged to meet with Mr Aloha at his house as he had something special to ask him in private. When he arrived, Tembani found him busy working in his garden. As soon as Mr Aloha spotted Tembani, his emotions were immediately triggered, and he broke down. He instantly put down the tool that he was using.

"Hello, Tembani," he said as tears started to roll down his cheeks.

"Hello, Mr Aloha," Tembani said as he walked briskly to greet him.

The two embraced each other for a considerably long time and were both in floods of tears, wailing like children. Mr Aloha then invited Tembani into his house for a cup of tea. Tembani felt very humbled by this invitation and accepted it.

When they entered the house, in his emotional state, Mr Aloha was still wearing his gum boots as he had forgotten to leave them outside. They made themselves comfortable in his lounge.

"How have you been, Tembani, and how is the business going?" Mr Aloha asked.

"Well, so far, the business is moving from strength to strength. I feel really blessed and can't complain. So, how are you keeping with yourself?" Tembani answered. "You've got a lovely garden out there, Mr Aloha. One of these days, I will come and help you with your gardening," he said.

"Anytime, Son. You are always welcome here," Mr Aloha said with a smile. "I just like to keep myself busy, and I spend a lot of time out there. So, how are your mum, brother and sister doing?" Mr Aloha asked.

"They're all doing great, thank you for asking," Tembani answered.

A hot drink was quickly made for Tembani, and as the two sat down to enjoy their drinks, Tembani explained his reasons for his visit.

"Thank you for the tea. It is really nice," Tembani said.

"You're most welcome," Mr Aloha replied.

"Right, Mr Aloha, I specifically asked to come and see you at your house to thank you for all the things you did for me whilst I was a student. I understand other teachers supported me, too, along the way, but in my eyes, you stood out in all that you did to support me. I would not be where I am today without you supporting what I was doing. I would like to offer my sincere gratitude for everything you have done," Tembani said.

"Tembani, you don't have to thank me. It was my duty as a teacher to make sure your passion for plants and flowers did not go unnoticed," Mr Aloha responded.

"I understand. Having teachers like you, who take their time to know individual students, is an amazing thing. You saw something special in me when, at the time, no one else thought it was anything special. At home, I had no father, and you embraced me as a son. The day you praised me and called me 'Son' made me feel very special, and from that moment on, you kind of represented a father figure I never had. You always checked up on me and made me feel valued and validated as a student and a person, for that matter. You built the foundation of my confidence in what I loved doing, and I cannot thank you enough. I thought it was right of me to come here in person to give my utmost gratitude to you," he said, but tears choked him from speaking clearly.

"Thank you so much, Tembani, for your words. Of course, as teachers, we're all there to support all our students, and I was only doing what I felt was right by you at that time," Mr Aloha said.

Tembani continued to praise his former teacher for seeing something special in him and believing in him when most doubted that his passion for plants and flowers would amount to anything.

"Don't forget, you were also the one that asked for my uniform size. For the first time, I felt dignified and loved myself. Wearing a new uniform gave me a sense of belonging, and I looked forward to coming to school every time. At least without feeling conscious of covering the torn parts of my uniform," Tembani said.

Mr Aloha repeatedly broke down as everything Tembani said seemed to overwhelm him. He had not expected anything back from him.

"Hey, Tembani, I was listening to your speech when you visited the school, and you touched on growing up without your father. If you don't mind me asking you, what is the situation now?" Mr Aloha asked.

"Thank you for asking. In fact, now that I am a grown man, I think it is only right for me to look for him. I would like to get to know him and understand why he left us when we were so young," Tembani replied.

"I am very pleased that you are not resentful about being brought up by your mother alone in his absence. I have total respect for you considering looking for your father. It takes guts and a brave man to do this. Good on you. Most children would grow up very angry and not even want to know their absent parent. This is an incredible thing you want to do. It is also important for your brother and sister, who I saw at your mother's birthday party, to know him too. It would be wonderful if you find him and have a man-to-man conversation. I will do whatever it takes to help you in your journey to find him," Mr Aloha said.

"Do you have any idea where he is or what he is doing?" Mr Aloha asked Tembani. "And have you expressed your intentions to your mother?"

"I have had a discussion with my mother before, when I was a student, but not recently," Tembani said.

"I think it's very important to talk to her about your intentions to find him before you start your search; just hear what she has to say. She might feel you didn't appreciate all the efforts she made raising you and your siblings alone," Mr Aloha said.

"Hell, no! I would not do anything to upset that woman. She worked so hard to look after us. I will certainly speak to her about this, and thank you again for your advice," Tembani said. "If I may ask, with your experience, do you have any idea how I can do this? I mean, look for him after I have talked to Mum?" Tembani asked.

"Yeah, I know of a programme I always watch on TV for long-lost families. If you're interested, you could contact them and see what happens. The programme has helped a lot of people like you to find their long-lost relatives," Mr Aloha said.

"Thank you very much for always sharing your wisdom with me and others. By the way, Before I forget, I have brought a small token for you. This is just to show my appreciation for your support, not just to me, but to all your students," Tembani said.

Tembani handed a token of his appreciation to Mr Aloha in the form of a cheque, but did not want him to open the envelope in his presence.

"You didn't need to do this, Tembani. I was only doing my job," Mr Aloha said.

"It's okay, Mr Aloha. It is my way of thanking you," Tembani said.

"Thank you very much, and bless your heart," Mr Aloha said.

Before leaving Mr Aloha's house, Tembani had a final bombshell to share with his former teacher.

"Before I go, I have something I would like to tell you," Tembani said.

"Why do I feel scared all of a sudden?" Mr Aloha said.

"Mr Aloha, I have been secretly working on opening a foundation to help others who have a similar upbringing to mine. I will also have other departments that would aim at helping those who would need the help that I offer. The million-pound question to you is, can I put this foundation under your name?" Tembani asked.

"Under my name? What do you mean?" he asked, seemingly shocked.

"I would like to name it 'The Aloha Foundation.' What are your thoughts?" Tembani said.

Mr Aloha just opened his mouth and placed his hand over it in utter shock at what he was hearing. He could not believe what he had just heard. He felt honoured by his former student to have a foundation named after him.

"Thank you so much, Tembani; this means a lot to me. I sincerely feel humbled and honoured for you to choose to name your foundation in my name. It is a huge recognition," he said.

"My pleasure, Sir. I feel you deserve this recognition. You are such a role model that we young people look up to," Tembani said.

"So what exactly is the foundation about again?" Mr Aloha asked. "Sorry, I am getting old and excited at the same time. I've forgotten what you have just said."

Tembani and Mr Aloha giggled.

"Under this foundation, I would like to support other children with a similar upbringing to mine, children from less privileged backgrounds and those with unique talents to fulfil their dreams and ambitions. I would also like to sponsor high-achieving students from underprivileged backgrounds to pay for their university tuition," Tembani explained, despite the fact that he was not academically gifted himself.

"I would also like to set up a horticulture project at my foundation for those students who have the same passion as mine. I want to encourage more students to become gardeners. There is a high market for this, and not many students find it attractive," he said with a smile.

"That's a great idea. We would like more people to share your passion. Flowers are beautiful; they have a lot of meaning. By the way, I liked your speech and the bit about the lotus flower. I didn't know how special that flower was," Mr Aloha said.

"Yeah, it is amazing indeed," Tembani said.

"I have been a teacher for so many years, and I have never seen anything like this. In my teaching career, I have been able to contribute and

UNFINISHED BUSINESS

make a difference in many student's lives, but not many have returned to share their stories. I'm so proud of what you want to do for your community. It is called giving back, and a lot of the students will certainly benefit from what you are going to offer," Mr Aloha said.

"Thank you, Mr Aloha. Take care of yourself, and we will catch up soon. I will also update you on how I get on with my search for my father," Tembani said.

Tembani bid farewell to Mr Aloha.

169

CHAPTER TWENTY-THREE
A significant meeting

When Tembani next met up with his mum, he had sent her a text telling her of his pending visit. He intended to break the news to her about his intention to find his long-lost father. As usual, she had prepared his favourite meal of spicy jollof rice and beef stew. She topped this with his other favourite, hot, home-baked bread. When Tembani arrived at his mother's house, he was very excited to see her.

"Hello, Mother, how are you?" Tembani asked.

"I'm very well, thanks, Son. How have you been? I haven't seen you for a couple of days; it seems like ages. How is business going?" Sindi asked.

"Business is good, keeping me on my toes. I have been attending meeting after meeting, and the orders are ridiculously high. It has been crazy. Most importantly, I have been very busy preparing for the launch of my foundation. But, hey, you know, Mum, that I wouldn't go more than a week without having your baked bread and soup, no way," Tembani joked with his mother.

"I know, and speaking of fresh bread, I've actually prepared some for you. It is in the oven. You know what? When that time comes," she winked at Tembani, "I'll have to teach your 'chosen one' how to bake a loaf," Sindi said.

"Mum! Please stop, stop, stop! Don't expect *that* from me any time soon; I am not ready and am too busy anyway," Tembani responded, rather embarrassed by his mother's suggestion for him to find a girlfriend.

"Okay then, I'll wait as long as it takes," Sindi joked.

"Mum, can I speak to you about something more serious, please?" Tembani asked. "You will need to be seated, and I hope you will not be offended by what I am about to tell you."

"Don't scare me, please. I hope everything is okay," Sindi said as she sat down, looking very tense.

"Oh yes, Mum, everything is fine. I met with Mr Aloha last weekend; remember my former teacher?" Tembani said.

"Of course I remember him. How is he doing? Is he still teaching, or has he retired?" Sindi asked.

"I guess he is nearing his retirement. I didn't ask him," Tembani said. "Mum, you know some time back, I asked you where my father was, and you told me what happened between the two of you, But I would like to find him and get to know him. I am a man now and not a boy. If I find him, it will be important to talk man-to-man and hear what he has to say for himself. I guess he deserves a chance to be heard. I have a lot of questions to ask him. What are your thoughts on this?" Tembani asked his mother.

"I am glad you've got to this point. I would love to support you to find him, but I really don't know where to begin. We haven't been in touch since the time he left home, and as you know, it has been a while. How do you intend to do this?" Sindi asked.

"When I visited Mr Aloha, we discussed this issue briefly, and he told me about a website where one can trace long-lost family members or loved ones. I would like to try the website. He said it was reputable for its services, and many families in my sort of situation have benefitted from this organisation," Tembani said.

"I truly hope everything goes well for you. I know how much this means to you," Sindi said.

"I'll do my best, Mum. I am not only doing this for me but for my brother and sister, too. We all deserve to know our father and that he gets to know us, too," Tembani said.

"I totally agree with you and wish you all the best. Keep me posted," Sindi said.

"Of course I will, and thank you for supporting me to do this," Tembani said.

He hugged his mother.

After this conversation, the whole family enjoyed a meal.

"Bro, when are you taking me shopping?" Thandiwe asked.

She had been acting like a little princess since she was six years old. She was spoilt rotten by her brothers as their only sister. Tembani always brought her new toys, plenty of clothes and shoes.

It took a while before Tembani was fortunate enough to find his long-lost father through the website Mr Aloha recommended.

The producers of the programme arranged for a special meeting between Tembani and his father at a local restaurant that was central to both of them. Both Tembani and Pilani were very anxious about this first meeting. They were not sure of what to expect from the other.

On the day of the meeting, Pilani arrived first at The Baringer restaurant and was very uptight to meet his son for the first time after so many years. The last time he had seen Tembani, he was ten years old. Before Tembani arrived, Pilani kept imagining what he looked like. His emotions were all over the place and got the better of him. He kept standing up and sitting down repeatedly. He was unsure of how Tembani would react to seeing him. He ordered a large glass of juice and subconsciously took huge gulps due to his nerves. In his mind, he expected his son to present with hostility and resentment towards him. He even imagined he might punch him. He expected the worst but was prepared for anything.

After a while, Tembani finally arrived at the restaurant. He briefly stood in the doorway and let his eyes wander from side to side. He looked for someone who resembled him, as his mother would always say, 'You look so much like your father,' Likewise, Pilani's eyes had not left the entrance, checking on everyone who walked in to see if it was his son.

At last, their eyes met, and instantly, they both knew they were father and son. Tembani looked the spitting image of his father; he was tall, dark and very handsome. Out of nerves, Pilani suddenly got up from his seat. He didn't know what to do with himself, whether to reach out to shake his son's hand or give him a hug. He was so confused. Instead, he just stood in one spot, waiting for whatever reaction Tembani would bring to the table. His heart was thumping, and so was Tembani's.

After a brief moment of confusion, Pilani braved to stretch out his hand to offer his son a handshake, but Tembani ignored him and did not reciprocate. This reaction did not really surprise Pilani; in fact, at that point, he thought Tembani was going to punch him in the face. His face started to twitch, and his hands were visibly shaking. Tembani was very calm even though his heart was beating faster than usual.

"Why don't you sit down?" Tembani said to his father.

Pilani sat down and greeted his son. "Hello, Tembani, I am Pilani, your father."

Tembani remained mute for some time.

"Thank you for coming to meet with me; I really appreciate it. I am sorry that it took this long," Pilani said.

"So you waited for all these years for me to look for you? If I had not made the effort, you would not have done? What kind of a father are you?" Tears started to roll down Tembani's cheeks, and his whole body started to tremble.

"Can I get you something to drink?"

"No, thanks, I'm good for now."

Watching this pain on his son's face also made Pilani's tears start to roll down his cheeks. He took out a handkerchief from his pocket and offered it to Tembani, but he refused to take it. Instead, he decided to use a table napkin to wipe his tears.

Pilani felt powerless at this point; he just rested his hands on both his cheeks in utter shame. He wished that the ground would just swallow him whole.

This moment was so unpleasant for both of them.

"Tell me, Dad, where have you been for all these years? No birthday cards from you for any of us. Nothing! Mum suffered alone looking after us. What do you have to say for yourself other than you were a very irresponsible parent? Don't just sit there, quiet. I wanted to meet you and get answers I've been longing for all these years."

"I am happy to answer you, Tembani, but today might not be ideal for that. We just met up, and clearly, our emotions are high. I would really like us to meet up again and talk man-to-man."

"What do you call this? Is this not man-to-man?"

"It certainly is, but there's a lot for me to talk about. I don't expect any sympathy from you for what I have done and put you all through, but you and your siblings deserve to know the truth about what happened between me and your mum. No excuse will be enough to explain the reasons I didn't reach out to you."

"Do you know how it felt as a child, growing up and not knowing who your father is? How embarrassing it was to go to school wearing a torn uniform amongst other kids? Being laughed at for not having things other children had? I was bullied for not having a father in my life, and that was a feeling that haunts me to this day. Do you have any idea? I taught myself to become a man!" Tembani raised his voice at his father.

"Tembani, you have every right to be angry with me. I am deeply ashamed and sorry for all the things that I have put all of you through. I can only wish I had been wiser and got help earlier; I would definitely have dealt with things differently. Again, I am sorry, Son," Pilani said.

"Unfortunately, lost time will not be recovered, and you cannot reverse this. Tell me, how will you make up for this? You neglected three souls and a wife. You left me as a boy, and now I am a man. Come on, Dad, whatever explanation you have better be reasonable. I mean it."

"You may not believe this; I thought about all of you every day, but it was not possible for me to get in touch. Can we arrange to meet up again soon so that I can explain my side of things? Please?"

"I'll have to think about it."

"Here is my number. Please call me and let me know when you will be free again for us to meet up. I truly appreciate your effort to find me. Before you go, how is Sipho and the young one? Is it a boy or girl?"

"My sister is now twelve years of age, Dad."

"What is her name?"

"Thandiwe."

"Beautiful name. Do you have any pictures of her on your phone now for me to just see what she looks like?"

"I don't think it will be a good idea for me to do that. I have to speak to Mum first and hear what she thinks. Maybe when we meet up next time."

"Fair enough. That's okay."

"Listen, Dad, I have business to attend to. Here is my business card, and all my contact details are on there. Let's catch up soon."

"Can I give you a hug?"

They give each other a brief shoulder-to-shoulder hug.

"Hope to hear from you soon," Pilani said.

"Okay," Tembani replied.

Both men leave the restaurant and go their separate ways.

CHAPTER TWENTY-FOUR
Long-awaited news for Sindi

Soon after meeting with his father, Tembani felt he owed it to his mother to tell her how it went. It had become a usual routine for Tembani to bring his mother fresh flowers on his visits to her, and she loved this.

"I would rather have this opportunity to smell the flowers now than when they are put on my grave where I can't smell them anymore," Sindi said.

"Wow, that's touching, Mum. Tell you what, you will live long to see your great-grandchildren."

Sindi laughed as Tembani gave his mum a cheeky wink.

"Fingers crossed. I guess you know what I will say next," she said.

"Please, don't. Let me enjoy my money before someone else comes into the picture."

"I'm just joking with you, my son. Take your time with matters of the heart."

"Trust me, I'll definitely take my time on that."

"So tell me, any updates on finding your father?"

"Thank goodness the results are positive. The website I used was very helpful, and I would recommend it to anyone looking for their loved ones. The team I worked with was amazing, and it was one of those experiences that you cannot express in words. Right, brace yourself, Mum, I've got great news. Did I just say great news? Well, I was able to find Dad, and we met at Baringer restaurant. You know that one on First Street, near Coombes station. I don't want to lie to you; it was an emotionally draining moment, and I can confess that I was a bit harsh with him at the start. He was not able to say everything he wanted to tell me because I didn't let him have that chance. I can also admit that inwardly, I was very pleased to have finally met him and see his face again."

"Oooh! I am so pleased for you, Tembani. Look, I have goosebumps all over. You finally got to meet with your father; that's so amazing. I can't believe I'm hearing this." Sindi was very emotional, and her hands started to shake.

"Mum, please, don't! You will set me off," Tembani said.

"How was he? Did he look well? Did he ask about Thandiwe?" Sindi asked question after question.

"Mum, please breathe. I know you are so excited I found your husband. In fact, he looked very well, sober and was dressed casually smart. But I have to say, I could not believe how similar in appearance we look,"

"I always told you that, haven't I?"

"Honestly, you were right. We look more like brothers than father and son. He's tall, just like me. Yep, he did ask about Thandiwe, and he wanted me to show him her photos on my phone. But I told him I needed to ask your permission first. I actually don't know what your thoughts are about it. When I told him her name, he said it was cute, and he liked it," Tembani said.

"Oh, bless him. It's so sad that he doesn't know his own child, let alone his only daughter, presumably. Anyway, I told you, you look like twins," Sindi said with a slight giggle.

"I beg your pardon? Twins? I'm far more handsome than him," Tembani said.

Sindi laughed. "Tembani, I am very pleased you put in all this effort to find your father. I just hope you and your siblings will be able to form a good relationship with him because he's been absent for a long time. So, when are you meeting with him again?"

"Well, we exchanged contact details, and I will reach out to him soon. I will certainly keep you in the loop. Mum, can I ask you a rather dodgy question?"

"Hmmmm...Go ahead, Temba," Sindi said hesitantly, unsure of what her son was going to ask her.

"Now that I have found my father, are you two ever going to get together or meet up?"

"Not any time soon. One thing at a time. For now, what is important is him getting to know you all and forming a father-child relationship. As far as me and him are concerned, time will tell. I will definitely not rush anything for now."

"Okay, I guess that makes sense."

Tembani waited for his young brother to come from school and spent some time chatting with his little sister, too, before he waved his good-byes.

A few weeks passed, and Tembani was ready again to reach out to his father. They arranged to meet up at the popular Moonlighting restaurant, known for serving continental cuisine. Both parties were better prepared emotionally this time and were more relaxed than in their previous meeting.

Tembani was the first to arrive at the restaurant and had booked a table for two. When Pilani arrived later, the waiter ushered him to their table. This time, they shared a father and son hug. It was still a bit awkward, but they were more accommodating to one another.

"Hey, Son, thanks for coming. Great to see you again."

"Thanks, Dad."

"How have you been?"

"Pretty good, and yourself?"

"I have been managing. So-so. How is your mum? Sipho and baby Thandiwe?" Pilani asked.

"They are all fine. Mum sends her greetings."

"Tell her I said thank you, and when you see her next, please send my greetings to her, too," Pilani said. "If anything, I really miss her cooking. She is such a brilliant cook and baker."

This was followed by an unexpected, awkward silence. Tembani gave his father this look that made him stop asking him about his mum. Pilani seemed to swallow a large lump out of fear of Tembani's reaction and quickly switched topics. He could not risk spoiling their relationship this early on.

"So, tell me, what are you doing now?" Pilani asked. "I could have asked you over the phone when I saw your business card. I didn't know what to think of it. How did you do at school?"

"I didn't do so well at school, but I now own T-S-T Flower Company, and I also grow plants of all kinds," Tembani replied.

"That's so amazing. What does T-S-T stand for?"

"Tembani, Sipho and Thandiwe."

"Wow, I am so happy for you! Congratulations on your achievements. How did this flower thing come about?" he said with an adoring smile.

"What do you mean?"

"The passion for flowers and plants?" he clarified.

"Well, it was just a natural thing for me. When I was growing up, I just found pleasure in looking after plants and flowers. I guess it was a coping mechanism that I adopted when growing up. One of my teachers at school spotted my talent and gave me an opportunity to look after the flowerbeds at the front of school. I did this very well, to the amazement of the headteacher, and one thing led to another.

"When I finished my GCSEs, the headteacher gave me a lot of plant and flower seeds to take home, and my passion kept growing from there. It was a long process, but I enjoyed every moment of it, and I got to educate myself on the types of flowers and their meanings. This helped me in their distribution to the right client and occasions," Tembani explained.

"This is super impressive, Son. Your story is so inspiring. I am actually moved. During my time as a teacher, I never experienced that kind of thing. I would never have imagined a love of flowers at school could lead anyone to achieve this success. I guess it is correct that if you give a child a tool, they can make something out of it. Well done for sticking to what you enjoyed and had a passion for."

"Thanks, Dad. But enough about me. So tell me everything I need to know from the moment you left home," Tembani asked his father.

"Of course, and I will start off by saying I am really sorry again for what happened between your mother and myself. Our relationship had become very toxic, and I was not in a great place in every way you can imagine. I was a bad father and husband. I did not treat your mother very well, especially when I was under the influence of alcohol. Looking back now, I pushed her to the limits, and it turned out to be a blessing in disguise that she was brave enough to ask me to leave the house. Losing my family and job knocked sense into my head and pushed me to find the help I needed."

Tembani listened carefully without interrupting his father.

"This is not an excuse by any means, but something you need to know is a little of my childhood. It was not great. I just want to paint the right picture for you from the start. My father was a man of 'tradition' and did not want to shift that perception. He believed he was always right. He brought me and my siblings up to believe a child was 'spoken at and not with' and never gave us a voice as children.

"When I was growing up, I was not given a choice to express myself. I only did what I was told. Going against my parents was a punishable offence where you would get a serious beating as punishment. The saying that 'the adult always knows best' was a very common saying in my family.

"To cut a long story short, my breaking point came when I was at secondary school. I was very good in almost all of my subjects, especially maths. My father then put pressure on me to become a mathematician just because of this, but I wanted to become a gamer. According to my father, this was not a smart decision and a decision that would cause him to be rebuked by his family. Apparently, all his family members were highly educated professors and lawyers, and he did not want any of us to bring disgrace to him.

"What other people thought of him outweighed what we thought. So, not being able to express myself built a lot of frustration inside me, but I could not find any outlet to express my feelings. I became an angry child. When I was at university, this anger within me spiralled out of control. I started to drink along with friends, but I gradually started to form a relationship with drink. I didn't realise this partnership between frustration and drink until it was too late.

"Every time I drank, I would feel happy and in control of things. Drinking helped me to forget all my problems for that short time, but it caused me the destruction of a lifetime. I lost everything. I was homeless at some point, until a good Samaritan offered to help me and referred me to a hostel. I have nothing to tell you that will make you proud of calling me your father, but on hearing your story, I can now say in reverse that I am proud to call myself 'your father.'

"I find it hard to say, but it's a blessing that my absence in your life turned out to be a blessing in disguise. If I had not left home, I can guarantee you that you would not have accomplished what you have today. Your mother always reprimanded me for repeating my father's behaviour, which I always criticised." Pilani gave this long speech to his son.

"Thank you, Dad, for this explanation. I came to this meeting equipped with anger, but having listened to you narrating your upbringing to me has made me have a different mindset. I am, in actual fact, very proud of you for bravely disclosing this difficult part of your childhood and also owning up to your own mistakes. It takes a great man to do this. So, where are you at now with your recovery?"

"Well, I have been in and out of hospital for alcohol addiction, but I am in a good place now. I have completed the whole detox programme, and I have not drunk alcohol for at least two years now. My health was failing me; my liver was almost gone. It was not worth it. I am currently taking a lot of medication to help me with the cravings, and I am managing," Pilani said.

"I see. I am really pleased that you got the support you needed," Tembani replied.

"Thank you, Son, for listening to me and not judging. It means a lot to me. Not every child in your position would have the same approach to give their parent another chance or even look for them. I am sincerely grateful," Pilani said, his eyes glistening with tears.

"No need to thank me, Dad. I am a grown man now and understand things better. It was crucial for me to give you this opportunity to hear your side of the story in your own words for closure. Can I give you a hug?" Tembani asked.

"Of course you can."

Pilani stood up and hugged his son. When they both sat down, Pilani had yet another revelation. This was the moment he had to say it all.

"In all of my growing up, would you believe me if I told you that I never in my life hugged my father as other children did with theirs? My father would never allow any of his children to hug him because this would be considered a sign of weakness. He never allowed us to be that close with him as he felt it was considered disrespectful for a child to be too close to their parent in that way," Pilani explained.

"That was some old generation thinking, Dad. I really feel pity for what you went through."

"It is what it is, but you can imagine how this impacts on a child's emotions. I grew up not knowing how to express myself. Crying and hugging were all considered signs of weakness. I was confused."

Tembani shook his head in disbelief at what his father had just disclosed.

"I am really sorry that I was not a good role model to you," Pilani continued, "but I am not ashamed to say that as my son, you are actually my role model. The first time I met you, I expected you to punch me in the face or even do worse, but you did not. You did not hang out with the wrong crowds because of my absence, but instead, you shifted your pains to focus on what has made you the successful man you are today.

"I credit your mother, who made such a difficult decision to kick me out even though she knew she did not go to work. She is such a strong woman who put the welfare of her children and her safety first. Not many women in her place would have made such a brave decision to lose the man paying the bills and putting food on the table. This was also a wake-up call for me because the problems I faced after she kicked me out worsened and forced me to get the support I needed. So I am actually grateful to her, but I pray that she will forgive me one day for the pain I caused her and shattering all the dreams we had when we first met."

"I am very pleased, Dad, that you now see things in that sense and are not angry with Mum for kicking you out."

"Believe me, I am thankful rather than resentful."

"Sorry to ask you a rather uncomfortable question. When you left home, did you have other children apart from us three?" Tembani asked.

"First of all, it is not an uncomfortable question but an expected one, and the answer to your question is no. I had no time to form any healthy relationships after my break up with your mum. Besides, I was in and out of hospital most of the time, going through the detox programme; it was impossible even to consider a relationship," Pilani said.

"I was just wondering if I had brothers or sisters out there," Tembani said.

"Well, you can rest assured you and your two siblings are the only children I have. So, may I sort of turn the question around? Are you in any relationship with anyone?" Pilani asked.

"Not yet! You are sounding just like Mum now. For now, I have other important things to focus my attention on, but soon. Anyway, to change the subject, I am launching a foundation, and I would like you to be part of it, if that's okay with you," he said.

"A foundation? That's a big thing to do, wow! Really amazing, my son, and what is the aim of your foundation?" he asked.

"To help other students with a similar upbringing to mine to get the right support, be it resources or financial. It will be a multi-purpose foundation. Interestingly, I will also offer a plant and flower apprenticeship for those who have the same passion as me," Tembani said with a smile.

"That is a very good cause, and I will certainly be honoured to be part of this. I wish you all the best with your foundation," Pilani said.

"I am glad you have accepted my offer because I aim to run a drug and alcohol department, and if you are happy to do this, I would ask you to be the head of that department. I am sure other families will benefit greatly from hearing your story and what challenges you had to face in overcoming alcohol addiction," Tembani said.

"Certainly, I would really love to share my story with other families. Not many fathers or people who have gone through what I have are given a fair chance to say their own side of story, and I am grateful you have given me this," Pilani said.

Tembani hinted at his intentions to arrange a meet-up between his mother and father to patch up their differences and for his father to be allowed to see his daughter Thandiwe, whom he had not met. He also wanted them to have closure between them.

Tembani acted as a mediator between his parents. Sindi was very pleased that her children had the chance to have the opportunity to bond with their father. Overall, Tembani was very pleased that both his parents were now on talking terms before the launch of his foundation.

It was crucial for Tembani to have both his parents present on this special occasion, and he wanted them to unite for the sake of him and his siblings. His parents agreed to meet on mutual ground. Sindi found it difficult to reconcile with her ex-husband, but agreed to be on talking terms for the sake of their three children.

CHAPTER TWENTY-FIVE

A foundation is launched

It took some time for Tembani's family to form a family bond, but this was achieved gradually. They had a lot to catch up with each other. Unfortunately, lost time could not be recovered.

At the entrance of The Aloha Foundation building stood two big statues on either side. One was of a woman holding a child to represent all single parents who bring up their children alone, and the other was a statue of a teacher kneeling down and speaking to a student wearing a torn uniform. This was in honour of his beloved teacher, Mr Aloha, and all other teachers who go out of their way to help their students who present with different talents and needs in schools.

On the day of the launch, all guests were mesmerised by the appearance of Tembani's building. His guests included the local mayor, who had cordially accepted his invitation, Mr Aloha, after which the foundation was named, Tembani's parents and his siblings, former teachers, former students and members of the community. The building was well decorated with immaculate flowers of all kinds and plants. The signature butterflies that once flew around his former school were also visible, flying gracefully above the building of his foundation. Tembani had also crafted an outstanding replica of a lotus flower and displayed it at the main gate to the foundation. He also included the lotus image in his company's logo, as he absolutely adored this flower and all it represents.

The ceremony was well attended. The weather was favourable, the sun shone bright, and the atmosphere was just beautiful. They were ushers at the gate who directed guests to their respective places. When everyone had sat down, Tembani addressed his guests with a well-prepared speech.

"A good afternoon to you all. I welcome you all to this special day: a day I never thought in my wildest dreams would be possible. Seeing all of you here makes me very happy, and I would encourage every child out there to believe in their dreams, as dreams can become reality. I would also like to say that without the support of my teachers and my mother, who was always there throughout my journey, this would have been impossible," Tembani said.

There was a great round of applause from the audience.

"First and foremost, I would like to invite our honourable mayor to come to the podium and officially launch the foundation," Tembani began. "Your Honourable Mayor, I welcome you."

Tembani bows his head to the mayor, and he stands up and walks towards the podium.

"Thank you so much, Tembani, for inviting me to this special occasion. It was my utmost pleasure to accept your invitation and to be part of your launch and its incredible cause. It is an amazing thing you have done for our community, and I wish you and your foundation great success. I have no doubt that many people will benefit from its cause. I would like to invite you and all the guests to come with me to the front of the building to cut the ribbon and officially launch The Aloha Foundation," the mayor said.

The whole congregation stood up and followed the mayor to the gate of the foundation.

After the mayor cut the ribbon, this was followed by a great applause and whistling to celebrate the official opening of the foundation. All the guests then walked back to their seats.

Tembani took his position again at the podium and explained his intentions to all his guests.

"Good day to you all again. As you are all aware, I am here to launch my foundation today. It is called *'The Aloha Foundation.'* I named it after my teacher, Mr Aloha, who is sitting over there. As much as I appreciate all the support I got from my teachers, Mr Aloha was a key reason for my success today. He spotted my passion and equipped me with the right support.

"The school gave me a great gift when I completed my education. Other children would have benefitted greatly from a certificate for great achievement in their subjects. My gift was a wheelbarrow full of pots with plants and flower seeds. I used this gift and developed myself, and I have proved to all of you that if you support a child's dream, no matter what it is, it can be successful." Tembani gave his heartfelt speech.

"First of all, I would like to say we need more of the Mr Aloha's who are not afraid to stand up for what is right. Teachers who are not afraid to be ridiculed by their colleagues for going the extra mile to support students like me. Teachers who do not use the same tool to measure students of different talents. Teachers who have a non-judgemental approach to the learning of their students. Thank you again, Sir, for changing my life, and I hope I can change another child's life and fulfil their dreams.

"My vision is to promote creativity in children and not division. The aim of my foundation is also to support people struggling with drugs and alcohol, a subject that is dear to me because my family was affected by this. My father, who has recovered from alcoholism, has requested a moment to address you all on this matter. Please, give him a round of applause," Tembani addressed the guests.

"A good day to you all," Pilani began. "As Tembani has highlighted, I requested a brief moment to address you all about my struggles with alcohol. I started drinking when I was eighteen and at university, initially to socialise with others, but gradually, it became more than just to socialise. With time, I noticed that I started to depend on alcohol for happiness and to cope with all my problems. I was not confident and comfortable talking openly about my childhood trauma.

"When I qualified as a mathematician and became a teacher, that is when I realised how unhappy I had become. Inside me, I knew this was not the passion I wanted to pursue. It was definitely not the dream I had chosen. I started to live someone else's dream and not mine. I became an angry man. As a married man, I took all my anger and frustrations out on those who cared and loved me. I became an abusive husband and everything I hated in my father. Alcohol took away my fears and my shame.

"Tembani, my son," Pilani said, facing Tembani, "I would like to thank you for taking that brave step to look for me. I would like to humble myself before everyone present. My son has taught me the meaning of love and that it is okay as a man to express your feelings and it's okay to cry.

"Today, I stand here at the opening of my son's foundation as a proud father. My son welcomed me back into his life without judging me, and I hope I will make him proud. My message to all the fathers out there who have left their children for different reasons is: please reach out to your children; they need you. Let them know that you love them despite the struggles you are facing.

"I admire my son's strength, his resilience and determination in life. My son has shown me the meaning of love, the meaning of forgiveness and what it means to be a family. Despite growing up without me in his life and enduring bullying at school, he persevered with his passion. He did not let my absence affect his focus on becoming the man he is today. It would have been easy for him to grow up as an angry child and mix with the wrong crowd.

"Lastly, I would like to thank my ex-wife for looking after our children in my absence, and this goes to all single parents out there who go out of their way to look after their children single-handedly. Thank you all for listening."

A loud clap from the audience is heard.

"Thank you, Dad, for that lovely speech." Tembani stepped up to the podium again. "I hope your testimony will help other fathers who are struggling with alcohol and other addictions. My father hopes that sharing his own experience will inspire others and give them hope that they, too, can recover from their drug and alcohol addictions.

"Lastly, I would like to say that I will also have a department to support children with different talents. The Aloha Foundation will offer scholarships to high-achieving students from families with little money. Most importantly, I will offer support to adults who dropped out of school for different reasons. My mother is a very intelligent lady, but she was not fortunate to complete her education due to poverty. Therefore, I have created a cooking and baking department, and I have no doubt that she will shine as the head of this department. She is a natural baker and cook. I will support her to develop her own cookbooks and share her skills with other mums who could not complete their education for different reasons," Tembani explained.

Mr Aloha had also been given the opportunity to speak on this day.

"Tembani, I would like to thank you for the huge honour of naming your foundation in my name. I don't believe I treated you any differently from other students. What I did for you, I would do over and over again for another student.

"I would like to encourage all of you students out there not to shy away from following your passions that are not academic. Even as a teacher, I am not oblivious to the fact that not every child is gifted academically. However, I believe every child deserves a chance to be recognised and acknowledged for who they are and whatever talents they present. Thank you all for listening and coming to support Tembani. Lastly, I can only hope that we will have many Tembani's in our schools," Mr Aloha said.

"And many Mr Alohas," Tembani concluded.

The audience applauded one final time to close the ceremony.

Sadly, despite Tembani's success and mediation between his parents, he was only able to unite his father and all his siblings. Unfortunately, his parents' relationship with each other could not be saved. However, Tembani found comfort in being able to forgive his father for his absence and continued to spread his message to those experiencing the same challenges as he did.

THE END

Printed in Great Britain
by Amazon

36683169R10112